PUFF

Smash!

Robert Swindells left school at the age of fifteen and joined the Royal Air Force at seventeen-and-a-half. After his discharge, he worked at a variety of jobs, before training and working as a teacher. He is now a full-time writer and lives with his wife, Brenda, on the Yorkshire Moors. Robert Swindells has written many books for young people, and in 1984 was the winner of the Children's Book Award and the Other Award for his novel *Brother in the Land*. He won the Children's Book Award for a second time in 1990 with *Room 13*, and in 1994 *Stone Cold* won the Carnegie Medal and the Sheffield Children's Book Award.

ROBERT
SWINDELLS

SMASH!

PUFFIN BOOKS

PUFFIN BOOKS

Published by the Penguin Group
Penguin Books Ltd, 27 Wrights Lane, London W8 5TZ, England
Penguin Putnam Inc., 375 Hudson Street, New York, New York 10014, USA
Penguin Books Australia Ltd, Ringwood, Victoria, Australia
Penguin Books Canada Ltd, 10 Alcorn Avenue, Toronto, Ontario, Canada M4V 3B2
Penguin Books (NZ) Ltd, Cnr Rosedale and Airborne Roads, Albany,
Auckland, New Zealand

Penguin Books Ltd, Registered Offices: Harmondsworth, Middlesex, England

First published by Hamish Hamilton Ltd 1997
Published in Puffin Books 1998
8

Set in Bembo

Made and printed in England by Clays Ltd, St Ives plc

British Library Cataloguing in Publication Data
A CIP catalogue record for this book is available from the British Library

ISBN 0–140–38280–1

I am indebted to Atif Imtiaz and David Swindells, who read this book in manuscript and made helpful suggestions.

ONE

Ashraf wiped the last smear of egg yolk off his plate with a morsel of bread, popped it into his mouth and gazed across the table at his sister. 'So, how much longer are you going to keep poor Stephen dangling, Abi?'

'Shut up, Ash, will you?' Abida cast a sidelong glance at their mother, placidly peeling an orange. They'd spoken in English and she hadn't latched on.

Their father was another matter. He cleared his throat and gazed at Ashraf over the top of the *Daily Telegraph*. 'What's this about dangling, Ashraf, and who is Stephen?'

Ashraf chuckled. 'Stephen's this lad at school, Dad. You've heard me talk about him. He's OK. He fancies Abi and she knows it because he told Colleen and Colleen told her.'

'And who exactly is Colleen?'

'She's Stephen's sister, Dad. She and Abi are in the same class.'

'I see. And I suppose you consider it cruel and unreasonable in your sister that she has not consented to accompany this young man to . . . er . . . raves and so forth? Am I right?'

Ashraf shrugged. 'Not really. I don't think he's even

asked her.' He grinned. 'He's a bit shy, old Steve.'

Mr Khan nodded. 'I'm delighted to hear it.' He treated his son to a basilisk stare. 'If at some time in the future, Ashraf, Stephen's shyness should wear off – and this *can* happen – I trust you will use your influence to see that he continues not to ask.' He blinked. 'I take it you receive my meaning?'

'Yes, Dad.'

'Good. And I'd be obliged if in future the two of you did not exchange banter in English when your mother is present. It is extremely rude to exclude a person from one's conversation by using a language she does not understand. Is that clear?'

Ashraf nodded. 'Yes, Dad.'

'Abida?'

'Yes, Dad. Sorry.'

'Hrrrmm.' Mr Khan disappeared behind his paper. Brother and sister exchanged grimaces. Their mother began breaking her orange into segments. It was a quarter past eight.

Two

At the same time in another part of Shadderton, Michael Crowley was also concealed behind a newspaper. He was Stephen and Colleen's father, and the paper he was reading at the breakfast table was the *Shadderton Post*. His voice issued from behind it. 'I see the council's approved the Millennium proposal. They'll need to get cracking if they're going to have it ready for January first in the year two thousand.'

'Two thousand and one,' grunted Stephen. 'The Millennium begins on January first, two thousand and one. Two thousand is the last year of the *twentieth* century because there was no year zero.'

'Clever clogs,' sneered his sister. 'The whole world's getting geared up to celebrate two thousand and my brother decides he'll leave it till the year after. It's absolutely typical.'

'Stephen's right though,' said their mother, buttering toast. 'It *ought* to be two thousand and one, but the powers that be have simply decided to bow to a misconception most people share.'

'See.' Stephen grinned. 'As usual the world's wrong and Stephen Crowley's right. Sometimes my genius terrifies me.'

'Well anyway, Shadderton's aiming at two thousand.' Mr Crowley folded the paper and laid it aside. 'So they've got – what? It's September now, so that gives them about fifteen months. Fifteen months in which to demolish most of the town centre and get the new stuff up. The Bennett Qureshi Millennium Development, they're calling it, after Alec Bennett and

Hanif Qureshi. They'll be lucky to have it ready in time.'

'Who're *they* when they're at home?' demanded Colleen.

Her mother looked at her. 'Alec Bennett was a famous playwright, love. Died sometime in the seventies, but he was born in Shadderton before the First World War. Surely you've done him at school?'

Colleen shook her head. 'Not that I remember. And what about whatsisname – Hamid Qureshi. Who's he?'

'Hanif dear, not Hamid. Hanif Qureshi. He was a novelist. Won a prize and they serialized the book on telly. Something about the sun. Then he was killed on a motorbike. Very young but already famous, and *he* was born in Shadderton.' She smiled. 'I suppose they're the only celebrities we've ever had, unless you count Corporal Coxmoor.'

'I know who *he* was,' said Colleen. 'His name's on the honours board at school. Won the VC in World War One, didn't he?'

Her mother nodded. 'Posthumously, at the battle of Ypres. Councillor Coxmoor's his grandson.'

'Hmmm.' Mr Crowley nodded. 'Old Coxmoor's dead against the development, you know. Waste of public money he calls it, even with the grant from the Millennium Fund. He reckons a monument of some sort'd be sufficient. In front of the Town Hall. Spend the rest refurbishing existing housing instead of knocking it down.'

'Boring,' growled Stephen. 'Anyway, half those houses are derelict and what about the abandoned mills? It's time they were pulled down.'

'Yes,' protested Colleen, 'but what about the houses that're still occupied? Where will the people go? Abi Khan's dad's got a shop there. What about *that*?'

Stephen's grin was malicious. 'It's not Abi and her dad you're bothered about,' he said. 'And it's not her mother either. It's Ash. You've got the hots for him and you make it dead obvious.'

'Stephen!' His mother glared. 'What sort of disgusting expression's *that* to use about your sister? Colleen is fifteen and I'm sure she hasn't got the *hots*, as you call it, for *any*body. Hots indeed.' She shook her head. 'I blame all this American stuff on TV.'

'It's true though,' pursued Stephen. 'Look at her face.'

'Stephen,' murmured his father dangerously, 'that's enough. It's twenty-past eight anyway, time you were both off to school.' He gazed at his daughter. 'And you'd better not let *me* catch you casting glances at Ashraf Khan or any other boy, young woman. There're important exams to pass before you start with any nonsense of that sort. D'you understand?'

'Yes, Dad.'

THREE

Basir Khan was seldom to be seen on foot in this part of Shadderton, and a few heads turned as the prosperous-looking businessman made his way unhurriedly towards the offices of Fixby and Walsh. As he approached the building, a white Jaguar turned across his path on to the tarmac pad in front of the five-storey cube of glass and steel, where it drew up and two men got out. These men had never shared a car before. Their dislike and distrust was mutual and they were usually to be seen glowering at each other across the floor of the council chamber. Now they strode side by side without speaking towards a pair of glass doors, converging with Khan as they did so.

'Salaam Aleikum,' murmured Khan, who had become acquainted with both men while serving on the Millennium Committee. The committee had had twelve members, and the only thing these three had in common was their opposition to the Millennium Proposal which had eventually been adopted by eight votes to four, the fourth dissenter being Stanton Fixby in whose office they had arranged to meet this morning.

'Morning,' mumbled Russell Pollinger, holding a

door for the other two. Kenneth Coxmoor said nothing in response to Khan's salutation, contenting himself with a barely perceptible nod. The three paused for a moment at the reception desk before proceeding to the lift which would whisk them to the third floor, where Mr Fixby would be waiting to conduct them to his office.

It was a large, impressive office, expensively carpeted and equipped with an antique desk whose leather top supported an array of state-of-the-art gadgetry and reminded Coxmoor of the flight deck of the starship *Enterprise*. Swivel chairs, luxuriously upholstered under glossy maroon leather, stood here and there on the burgundy carpet. Good pictures adorned the walls, and a large window afforded a panoramic cross-town view to fields and hills beyond.

The four men sank into chairs. Coffee was brought. Russell Pollinger sought permission and lit a cigarette. Stanton Fixby leaned forward, jabbed a button and spoke into a gadget. 'No calls, no callers. I'm unavailable till two thirty.' He sank back, folded his arms and smiled at his three visitors. 'So, gentlemen,' he purred. 'Let's get down to business, shall we?'

FOUR

'Right.' Mr Greenglass rubbed his big, red hands together and grinned wolfishly at his A level English class. '*Middlemarch.*' He held up his copy of the novel. 'What's it about, eh?' A hand shot up. 'Yes, Justin?'

'About nine hundred pages, sir.' Justin Case, class clown, got the laugh he sought but not from the teacher, who nodded and said, 'Nine hundred pages exactly, Justin, making it the thickest object in the room after yourself.' This got a bigger laugh and the clown, blushing furiously, shrugged and dropped his eyes.

The teacher turned, scrawled a sentence on the board and stood back. 'What d'you think Eliot meant when she wrote this?' He glanced about the room. 'Anybody?'

Ashraf read the sentence. *Destiny stands by sarcastic with our dramatis personae folded in her hand.* He frowned, read it through again and raised his hand.

Greenglass gazed at him. 'Yes, Ashraf?'

'Sir, I think . . . I think she meant, like, people have ideas about how their lives will work out, but they're nearly always wrong because destiny – destiny makes stuff happen that they can't predict, like an accident or something that changes everything.'

The teacher nodded. 'Good answer, Ashraf. Excellent in fact. Can anybody give me another word for destiny? Yes, Tracey?'

'Fate, sir?'

'Fate'll do nicely, Tracey. Thank you.'

The lesson proceeded. Stephen gazed out of the window. Destiny. He smiled faintly to himself. It'd mess up Dad's predictions all right if destiny shoved Colleen into Ash's passionate arms and Abi into mine. Yeah. His smile broadened. That'd *really* be something to write about.

FIVE

Rehana Majid was eight. At three fifteen that Thursday afternoon, she collected her four-year-old brother Shofiq from his nursery class as usual. The pair held hands as they left the schoolyard and made their way through a succession of shabby streets towards Khan's, where Rehana was to buy flour and a tin of bangun for her mother. There was a five-pound note in a zip-pocket of her green backpack.

As the two children turned into Alma Street, a boy of about fourteen stepped out of a derelict house in front of them. A second boy stood watching from the doorstep as his companion jerked his head towards Rehana's pack. 'What you got in there?'

'Just my lunchbox,' said Rehana. 'And a book and a pencil case.'

'What – no money?'

The girl shook her head. 'No.'

'You're a liar, same as all Pakis.' He held out a hand. 'Let me see.'

Rehana shook her head. 'No.' She wrapped her free hand round the strap of her pack. 'Let us pass, please. I have to go to Khan's.'

The boy leered. 'What, without dosh? Started giving stuff away has he, old Khan?' His face grew suddenly fierce. 'Gimme that backpack before I rip it off your back, Paki.' The boy on the step guffawed. Rehana swallowed. Shofiq started to sniffle.

The boy glanced at the infant, then at Rehana. 'I bet you'd be in serious bovver if something happened to the kid, wouldn't you?'

Rehana nodded, looking at the ground. The boy shrugged. 'Well, you know what to do, don't you? Gimme the dosh and nothing'll happen. 'Seasy.'

Rehana let go Shofiq's hand, shrugged off the pack and unzipped the pocket. She held out the note. The boy snatched it and shoved it in his pocket. 'Any more?'

Rehana, close to tears, shook her head. 'That's all. It was only for flour and –'

'Ugh!' The boy screwed up his face. 'Paki grub.

Don't talk about Paki grub, kid. Listen.' He darted forward, seized the girl's lapels, lifted her clear of the ground and thrust his face into hers. 'You never seen me, right? Me and my mate here. This never happened. You were messing with that fiver and you lost it down a drain or it blew away or some kid at school nicked it. Pick any lie you fancy, only not a word about us or we'll be back for the kid. Goddit?'

'Yes,' gasped Rehana, half-throttled. The boy let go and she fell, striking her chin on the pavement. As the two lads ran off Shofiq squatted, plucking at his sister's coat, trying to raise her.

SIX

Friday morning. A chill in the air, but hazy sunshine hinted at warmth and drowsy wasps later. Swinging down the road with their bags, Stephen and Colleen met Abida and Ashraf coming out of Alma Street. It wasn't an arrangement but it happened a lot. The two girls exchanged smiles and fell into step side by side, but Stephen's jokey inquiry as to whether his friend had finished *Middlemarch* yet drew only a grunt from Ashraf. Hands in pockets they strolled behind their chattering sisters and Stephen tried again. 'OK for the match tomorrow, Ash?' Shadderton United were playing at home and the two lads sometimes went together.

Ashraf shook his head. 'Don't think so.'

'They're playing Fulham. It'll be a good match.'

'Probably. I won't be there though.'

'Hey.' Stephen glanced sidelong at his friend. 'What's up, Ash?'

'Nothing.'

'Aw, come *on* – something's bugging you, I can tell.'

'Leave it, Steve.'

'No. We're friends. You can tell me.'

'OK, Steve.' Ashraf stopped and faced him. 'Last night, two white lads attacked the daughter of one of my dad's customers. She's eight years old. They robbed her and left her unconscious on the pavement and her four-year-old brother crying his eyes out, all for a fiver. That's why I'm a bit quiet this morning, and that's why I won't be coming to the match with you.'

Stephen pulled a face. 'Yeah, well . . . that's tough, Ash. It's awful but I mean, why freeze me out? *I* wasn't there. I wasn't one of 'em. Is the kid . . . is she OK?'

Ashraf shrugged. 'She's in hospital. Concussed. Stitches in her chin. Scarred for life, probably. And you *are* one of them, Steve, whether you like it or not. You're white, I'm Pakistani. Paki to you.'

'That's not fair!' cried Stephen. 'Paki's a word I never use. Never. You were born here, same as me. We're British.'

'Ah, but you see it's not nationality that counts. It's race, Steve. Colour, when you come right down to it.'

Stephen was about to protest further when Abida and Colleen approached. They'd noticed the boys weren't behind them and turned back. 'What're you playing at, you two?' demanded Colleen. 'You're going to make us late.'

'We're . . . arguing, I suppose,' said Stephen. 'Ash has suddenly decided I'm racist.'

Ashraf shook his head. 'I didn't say that.' He looked at his sister. 'Steve was wondering why I'm not my usual jokey self this morning, so I told him about Rehana Majid. What those whites did to her.'

'Ah. But did you also tell him about the woman, Ash? The *white* woman who found Rehana, administered first aid, got somebody to call an ambulance and then took little Shofiq home? Did you mention her at all?'

'Well no, but –'

'But nothing, big brother. If you're going to tell a story you must tell it all, otherwise it gets twisted out of shape.' She smiled at Stephen. 'Don't look so solemn, Steve. He's always been moody, my brother. He'll be over it by breaktime. Come on.' They walked east, to where the sun was a fuzzy orange ball over Shadderton Comp.

SEVEN

Saturday, two fifty-five. Stephen in jeans, leather jacket and United scarf spotted the shortest queue at the turnstiles and joined it. It was the shortest but it wasn't short and it wasn't moving much either. He glanced at his watch. Four minutes to kick-off. 'Get a flipping move on,' he muttered. 'We'll be two up by the time I get in at this rate.'

There were still three people ahead of him when the famous Valley roar told him the game had commenced. 'Come on!' he shouted, standing on tiptoe to see the guy in the kiosk. 'What is it – tea break or something?' The man ignored him, scooping up money and working the stile in a slow, mechanical rhythm. Another fan was admitted, then another. Stephen listened to the crowd, praying there wouldn't be a goal before he got inside. He was almost there, dancing with impatience, when the lad immediately in front of him turned, looked past his shoulder and yelled, 'Hey, Karim, Ishaq!' Two youths were pelting across the car park. Panting and grinning, they shoved Stephen aside and thrust notes and coins into their friend's outstretched hand. He slapped the money on the counter. 'Three please.'

'Hey!' protested Stephen. 'There's a flipping queue, you know.'

The arrivals eyeballed him and one growled, 'Want to make something of it, do you?' The stile clicked as the first youth passed through. Stephen shrugged. 'There's a queue, that's all I'm saying. You join a queue at the end, not the middle.' He wished this *were* the middle – that there were fans behind to back him up, but he was the last.

'*We* don't,' sneered the lad who had challenged him. 'We join where we like. C'mon, Ish.' They turned their backs on him and pushed through the stile.

It was still goalless when Stephen got in. Four people had to stand to let him pass. He took his seat and looked around for the three Asians but couldn't see them. He'd just settled to enjoy the game when the four he'd disturbed were up again and a heavy guy of about eighteen came crabbing along the row and plonked down beside him. Immediately he leaned towards Stephen and muttered, 'I saw what them three Pakis done to you, kid. I'd've smashed 'em only I was in another queue.'

Stephen shrugged. 'Doesn't matter. We're all in now. Didn't miss much.'

'Not the point though, is it? Our Ground. Our town. Our *country*, see? *And* we invented the game.'

'Never mind,' mumbled Stephen. 'I'm not bothered. And it's their country too. Born here.'

'Bollards!' The man grabbed a handful of Stephen's

sleeve. 'Listen, kid. Don't matter where he's born, a Paki's a Paki. Even if his bleedin' *granny* was born here, he's still a Paki. You give 'im an inch, he'll take a flipping mile. I know. I've studied 'em.'

This guy doesn't look the student type, thought Stephen. *I wish he'd belt up and let me watch the game.* Aloud he said, 'Leave it, OK? White fans do the same, or worse. It's to do with soccer, not race.' He freed his sleeve with a jerk. The man tutted, shaking his head. 'There's too many like you, kid. That's why the country's falling apart. Here.' He thrust something into Stephen's side pocket. 'Read that when you get a minute. It tells the truth, not like the bleedin' papers.'

To Stephen's relief, the man left him alone for the rest of the half. At half-time he queued for a hot pie then found a seat in another part of the stand. He didn't see the man again, nor the three Asians. United won one nil but he hadn't enjoyed the game. He wished he'd stayed home, like Ash.

EIGHT

'Prats.' Stephen spoke the word aloud, lying on his bed. He'd locked himself in his room straight after tea, brooding over the turnstile incident. The ceiling was

16

a screen on which he saw the mocking faces of the three youths, and there was a sound track. *Want to make something of it, do you?* It was to drown this out that he'd spoken aloud.

'Wish I *had* made something of it,' he murmured. 'I *should* have.' *One against three?* whispered common sense inside his head. *Get real, Steve.*

'Yeah, OK, but I didn't do anything when Ash practically blamed me for what happened to the Majid girl either, did I? I let him get away with it.'

He rolled on to his side and saw his jacket on the chair-back. There was a bulge where the heavy guy had shoved something in the pocket. *Read this when you get a minute.* What is it, the latest edition of *Viz*?

Out of curiosity and because he was arsed off brooding, Stephen got up, fished in the pocket and pulled out a crumpled leaflet. He laid it on the bedside unit and smoothed it out. Across the top in bold red capitals was the word BLACKOUT. Under this were ten short paragraphs of close red type. Behind the print, covering the entire leaflet, was a black and white photo of what looked like some sort of riot – screaming black faces, upraised arms, sticks being waved. Stephen switched on the lamp, slid the leaflet into the pool of light and read the first paragraph:

There are now more blacks in Britain than Maoris in New Zealand, and thousands more are born each year. Unlike the

Maoris, these people are not in their own country. Their presence puts an intolerable strain on our National Health Service, as well as causing unemployment and a shortage of housing.

'Not to mention longer queues outside football grounds,' muttered Stephen. His eyes slid down to the next paragraph.

A number of white patients have become infected with sickle-cell anaemia after receiving blood donated by blacks, and a woman in Birmingham gave birth to a black child after a transfusion from a black donor.

'Rubbish!' He didn't read on but turned the leaflet over. More red print. This time the background showed dozens of black infants sitting on the floor of a nursery classroom. He scanned the print, which was larger on this side and more widely spaced.

Year by year our country is being swamped and taken over by people who don't belong here. Successive governments do nothing. BLACKOUT is an organization of concerned Britons determined to fight this creeping menace – a menace which threatens not only our heritage but our very lives and the lives of our children. If you care – if you want to help us smash the black threat – fill in the coupon below and mail it to the address at the bottom of this leaflet, or phone us on . . .

The number had a Shadderton code. Stephen scoffed. 'Organization! There's probably about six of 'em.' He went to drop the leaflet in the waste-paper basket, changed his mind and slipped it into his drawer. 'I'll show this to Ash sometime,' he murmured. 'I'll say if *I'm* racist, what would you call *these* guys?'

NINE

'Waseem.' Ashraf's father stood up as his wife's brother's son entered the room. 'How good to see you. Your father – is he well? And your mother?'

'They're both fine.' Waseem shook his uncle's hand and glanced towards his aunt. 'Yourselves?'

'We're well, thank you. Come, sit down. Abida – some tea for your cousin, please.'

Abida got up and left the room. Her mother followed. Waseem sat down. 'Where's Ashraf, Uncle?'

'In his room,' said Hassan. 'Homework, you know.'

'Ah.' At twenty, Waseem had left homework behind to join his father in the motor-repair business. 'How's the Majid child – Rehana, isn't it?'

Hassan nodded. 'Rehana, yes. She's home. Stitches in her chin. Still shaken, her father tells me. Doesn't wish to return to school.'

'I don't blame her.' Waseem stared into the gas fire. 'Her attackers, I suppose they haven't been found?'

Hassan shook his head. 'Not that I've heard.'

'I didn't think so. The police don't look very hard when the victim is one of our people.'

His uncle frowned. 'I'm sure they do all they can, Waseem.'

The younger man was about to reply when Ashraf walked into the room. 'Waseem,' he beamed, 'I thought it was you.'

His cousin looked severe. 'I hope you're not neglecting your homework on my account?'

'Would I do a thing like that?' asked Ashraf.

His cousin nodded. 'I think so.' They both laughed. Zainab and Abida came through from the kitchen with tea and sweets. Zainab set everything out on two small tables, then withdrew. Abida stayed.

'So.' Waseem sipped from his cup and smiled at Abida through the steam. 'How are things with you, little cousin?'

'I'm not little,' pouted Abida. 'I'm fifteen and things are OK, thanks.'

'Good. Not been mugged or anything?'

'Mugged?' The girl looked puzzled. 'Why d'you ask that, Waseem?'

Her cousin pulled a face. 'It happens, little cousin, more and more. The authorities do nothing.'

'Perhaps', ventured Abida, 'it'll get better when the Millennium Development's built.'

Waseem gazed at her. 'Why should *that* make any difference?'

Abida shrugged. 'Well, you know – wider streets, better houses. The most up-to-date facilities for everybody to share. Even the name – the Bennett Qureshi Millennium Development. It's meant to bring people together, and I think it will.'

Her cousin shook his head. 'It won't, Abida, believe me. And anyway that's not the way to go. What's needed – what *our* people need – is separate facilities. Schools especially. In fact –' He glanced at his uncle. '– that's really why I called, to tell you about a group that's being formed here in Shadderton to fight for the things we need.'

Hassan frowned at his nephew. 'Fight?'

'Well, press for,' amended Waseem. 'Demand. Use whatever word you prefer, Uncle, but it's time we stopped waiting for the powers that be to help us and took matters into our own hands. That's what Khalifa's all about.'

Hassan cleared his throat. 'I don't know what Khalifa is, Waseem, and I don't think I want to know. One thing I do know is this – there's more than enough trouble in the world already without our forming groups to cause more.' He stood up. 'It was good of you to call, Nephew. Carry our good wishes to your parents, won't you?'

Waseem got to his feet looking both angry and embarrassed. 'Very well, Uncle, since you insist, I'll go, and yes I *will* give your good wishes to my parents. And perhaps the next time some child is beaten up and robbed on its way to your shop, the police will actually apprehend those responsible, but I doubt it.' He strode towards the door.

'Hang on.' Ashraf stood up. 'I'll walk with you part of the way.'

Hassan looked at his son. 'Ashraf . . .'

'It's OK, Dad, I need some air, that's all.' The cousins walked out of the room. Father and daughter followed with their eyes. Zainab came in and began clearing the tables. The sweets had hardly been touched.

TEN

'Our parents' generation is locked in the past,' said Waseem as he and Ashraf took the path across the recreation ground. 'They behave as though we're still a subject people. You know – accept whatever comes without complaint. Everything passes, so bow your head and shuffle by, it's all you can do. Pah!' He turned his head aside and spat into the grass. 'It's all we've done for the last two hundred years and look where it's got us. We daren't let our children out of our sight in case some brainless moron's waiting to pounce. Well –' He placed a hand on Ashraf's shoulder. '– it's our turn to pounce, cousin Ashraf. Our turn.'

Ash glanced at him. 'What exactly *is* Khalifa, Waseem? Do you have . . . you know, a leaflet or something?'

The older man shook his head. 'No leaflet. Let other organizations waste their time and funds producing leaflets. Do you know where the Asian Youth Movement has its headquarters?'

Ashraf nodded. 'It's the three-storey building on the corner of Ladysmith Street and Westgate, isn't it?'

'Right. There's a meeting, seven thirty Monday night in room two. Be there if you're interested. You'd better go back now.' They halted. Waseem looked at his cousin. 'Better not mention the meeting at home, Ash. Make some excuse. Seeing a friend. Anything. You'll come though?'

Ashraf nodded. Waseem grinned and punched him in the arm. 'Way to go, kid. See you Monday.'

'See you.' Ash stood for a moment, watching his cousin cross the road and stride off into the dusk. Then he turned and walked slowly back across the rec.

ELEVEN

Mr Greenglass peered down at his notes, then up at the class. 'Last Thursday we considered the question, what is *Middlemarch* about? And we decided it wasn't about just one thing. We said that the novel contains a number of themes, and we looked at one in particular. Will somebody remind us which one?'

'Sir, he's not here.'

The teacher scowled at Justin Case. '*Who's* not here?'

'Will Somebody, sir.' The class tittered. Mr Greenglass gazed at the clown. 'How far have you got with reading *Middlemarch*, lad?'

'Sir, I'm on page thirty.'

'Very good, Justin. Most impressive, until we realize that the novel doesn't begin till page twenty-nine. What are you doing after school today?'

'Circuit training, sir. Soccer team.'

The teacher shook his head. 'No, Justin, that's what you *were* doing. What you'll actually do is report here at three thirty clutching your copy of *Middlemarch*, read chapter one and then produce me an essay on the character of Miss Dorothea Brook in your very best handwriting on at least two sides of A4 paper.'

'But sir . . . Mr Dawson'll be expecting me.'

'Your mother expected you for nine months, lad. I'll speak to Mr Dawson. You just make sure you're here at three thirty on the dot.'

The boy looked stricken. 'It's the first match Saturday, sir, and I'm on the team. Mr Dawson'll drop me if I don't train.'

'If that happens, Justin, you'll have only yourself to blame. You can't expect to be the class clown *and* a soccer hero. You are free to choose, but not until you've written my essay. Now –' He looked around the class. '– who's going to remind us which theme we looked at last Thursday? Yes, Timothy?'

'Sir, defeated aspiration as shown in the stories of Doctor Lydgate and Dorothea Brook.'

'Excellent. Give us another word for aspiration, Bradley.'

'Uh – *hope*, sir?' ventured Bradley Mattock.

Greenglass nodded. 'Hope, yes. Ambition perhaps. And to what does Dorothea aspire . . . er . . . Sharon?'

Ashraf switched off, letting his thoughts take their own direction. He was thinking about the meeting tonight, and about aspiration. Moulding the people of Shadderton into a single community. *That's* an aspiration, isn't it? Snag is, not everybody wants it. Waseem doesn't for a start. Khalifa doesn't. So what happens when somebody's aspiration clashes with somebody else's? The question made him uneasy and he wondered whether it might be best to skip the meeting. Trouble was he'd promised, and a promise is a promise.

TWELVE

Five past twelve. Stephen and Bradley stood in the lunch queue. Kids sat at long tables chewing, chatting, slurping Coke.

'Didn't see you at The Valley,' said Bradley.

Stephen shrugged. 'I was there.'

'Good win.'

'S'pose so, yes.'

'How d'you mean, s'pose so? Course it was. Perfect start to the season.'

'Hmmm.' Stephen chose veal-and-ham pie and salad. 'It's away form that counts. Think they'll beat Bradford City, Saturday?'

'Course.' Bradley selected fish and chips. They shuffled towards the puddings, sliding their trays.

'You going?'

Stephen shook his head. 'Too far.'

'Part-time supporter.' They took stewed pears and custard and carried their trays to a table which was unoccupied except for Justin Case, who was chomping on a sandwich and reading a fat book propped against the water jug.

'Hey up, Justin.' Bradley unloaded his tray. 'What you reading? Something mucky I bet.'

'What d'you *think* I'm reading, you donkey?' growled Case. 'Gotta do that flipping essay for Greenglass, haven't I?'

'Well –' Bradley sat down. '– you will insist on playing the clown.'

Stephen grinned. 'Good though. *Will Somebody*. Wish I could think 'em up.'

'Why?' muttered Justin. 'So you can spend *your* lunch-breaks reading flipping *Middlemarch* and getting indigestion?' He jerked his head at the book. 'I reckon they choose 'em by weight, just to keep us busy.'

Bradley nodded. 'Could be right. You travelling Saturday? Bradford?'

The clown nodded. 'Yeah, *if* I ever finish this flipping chapter with you two nattering on.'

'Oh, sorry.' Bradley winked at Stephen. 'Not used to dining with bookworms, me and Steve.'

Stephen smiled, thinking, Justin Case. What sort of parents land their kid with a name like that? Must run in families, clowning.

THIRTEEN

On the wall was a brown arrow with ROOM TWO stencilled on it. It directed Ashraf to a flight of dusty wooden stairs which creaked as he ascended. At the top was a dim, bare landing and two doors, one closed, one open. He peered through the open door. Chairs of canvas and tubular steel had been arranged in six rows of five facing a battered table. Of the thirty seats only seven were occupied, all by young men. Waseem wasn't there. Behind the table, on rather more substantial chairs, sat two older men, neither of whom was known to Ashraf. He took an end seat on the back row and looked at his watch. Seven thirty exactly. Where was Waseem?

One of the men behind the table got to his feet. 'Er . . . I know it's seven thirty, but I think we'll wait five minutes in case . . .' He looked at his companion, who nodded. Muted groans came from the seven young men, who seemed to know one another. The man who had spoken scowled in their direction and sat down just as Waseem walked in.

Ashraf attracted his cousin's attention with a raised hand and Waseem came over. 'Budge up, kid.' Ashraf moved on to the next seat and his cousin sat down. 'Sorry I'm a bit late. Rush job at work. Any trouble at home?'

Ashraf shook his head. 'I said I was off down the library to read up on *Middlemarch*.'

'On what?'

'*Middlemarch*. It's a book.'

Waseem smiled. 'Sounds like a time of year. Hiya, Karim – all set?' The question was addressed to one of the group in front, who had twisted round in his seat. He nodded. 'All set.'

'Good,' said Waseem. The youth turned away.

'Who's he?' whispered Ashraf.

'Karim Majid. Brother of Rehana and Shofiq.'

'Ah.'

There was a sound of feet on the stairs. Two middle-aged men appeared, taking seats near the door. The man who had spoken before now stood up again. 'It's nearly twenty to eight so we'll get started.' He rubbed his hands together, glancing down at a square of card on the table. 'I want to begin by thanking all of you who have taken the trouble to attend what could prove to be ... ah ... a very important or even historic meeting here in Shadderton tonight.'

The man's tone betrayed his disappointment. He'd prepared his little stack of cue cards with a more impressive audience in mind. He cleared his throat. 'For far too long our little community has suffered discrimination, abuse and harassment, and for far too long we have shrugged our shoulders saying, "We are a non-white minority, it is to be expected." And what have we found, hmm? What lesson have we learned?' He gazed at his meagre audience. Nobody responded so he ploughed on, answering his own question. 'We have learned that those who tolerate intolerance get more intolerance.'

'Yeah!' cried one of the seven youths, and his companions joined in with grunts and nods.

Encouraged, the speaker leaned forward, propping himself on his knuckles. 'Since it seems passivity serves only to enrage certain elements, some of us feel that it is time to stop being passive. That it is time to stand up for ourselves, and for our children.' Looking at Karim Majid he repeated, softly, 'And for our children.'

Majid stood up and walked to the front. The speaker rested a hand on the youth's shoulder. 'Our brother here has a story. A sad and a frightening story. Listen to what he has to say, because it concerns something that could happen to your daughter, your little sister, your baby brother, tomorrow or the day after, right here in Shadderton. Go on, Karim. We're listening.'

'Everybody knows it already,' whispered Ashraf. 'It was in the *Post*.'

'Ssssh!' hissed Waseem. 'That's not the point. Listen, and watch.'

FOURTEEN

Majid began nervously but warmed to his subject. At first his audience listened in silence, but as he grew more eloquent they were stirred to indignation, then to anger, then to passion. The group he'd come with muttered, growled and shouted. The two latecomers began by nodding approval and progressed to sitting forward, fists clenched on knees and eyes on the youth's face, breathing oaths and imprecations. Even Ashraf, who'd heard every detail of the story before, felt a surge of fierce emotion which drove him to his feet as Majid came to the end of his speech. Only Waseem remained calm, watching the reactions of the others with quiet satisfaction.

When the noise died down, the man behind the table rose and nodded to Majid. 'Thank you, brother, for that eloquent . . . that *timely* contribution.' He waited as the youth, flushed and perspiring, resumed his seat amid the acclamation of his friends, then leaned forward and spoke softly. 'It is clear to me that everybody in this room is moved by a deep sense of indignation at what we have just heard. *I* am moved. Each one of us wants to do something about it, but what?

What can we do?' He paused as the man beside him stood up, then continued, 'This gentleman is Mr Mohammad Iqbal from Birmingham, where people – ordinary, decent people like you and me – *are* doing something about it. Mr Iqbal has travelled a hundred miles today to tell us what they are doing, and to show us how *we* might do the same. Mr Iqbal.'

There was no passion in Iqbal's speech. No rhetoric. He spoke in a matter-of-fact way about organization, recruitment, fund-raising. He talked about the need to politicize, to raise the awareness of thousands of people he said were out there, straining at the leash to act but not knowing how because they lacked leadership. The sort of committed leadership tonight's audience might provide if the will was there, which he felt certain it was. He spoke of the growing threat posed by white extremists, and of the urgent necessity of building a mass party to oppose and to smash it. 'I am not at all discouraged', he concluded, 'by the small size of tonight's audience. I have addressed small gatherings many times before, and each time I have reminded myself that in nineteen twenty-three the German Nazi party had only a handful of members, and that ten years later it came to power with a membership in the millions.' He permitted himself a thin smile. 'It seems to me that what the little white corporal did, we might hope to do also, Ins'allah. Thank you for your attention. Goodnight, and good luck.'

FIFTEEN

'Hey look, Abida – they've started.' Colleen pointed. A derelict mill they passed every morning was now enclosed in a grid of scaffolding. The pavement in front of the building had been roped off and some men were stripping slates from the roof. A chute of yellow plastic tubing had been rigged between the roof and a heavy truck parked below. Slates tossed into the mouth of this tube fell eight storeys to land with a crash in the bed of the truck.

Abida nodded. 'I know. My dad got a letter from the council yesterday. Compulsory Purchase Order.'

'What does that mean?'

'It means the council's buying the shop so it can be knocked down.'

'But . . .' Colleen looked at her friend. 'How . . . I mean, what're you going to do then? About making a living?'

Abida shrugged. 'We get a council flat till the development's finished, then Dad will be offered shop premises in the new centre.' She pulled a face. 'If we can afford the rent.'

'Doesn't seem fair,' said Colleen, 'messing people's

lives up like that. Will these new shops have living accommodation?'

Abida nodded. 'I think so, but that's not the problem. Most of our customers are Asian, see? They live all around us. Dad's worried that when they demolish the houses, the people will be scattered all over Shadderton and his place won't be handy for them any more.'

As the girls swerved into the road to avoid the roped-off stretch, a volley of shouts and wolf whistles made them look up. Demolition men in silhouette against the sky, waving and wiggling their hips. Abida flushed and dropped her eyes. Suppressing her own embarrassment Colleen grinned and waved back, provoking a fresh volley, and at that moment Ashraf strode up looking furious. Overhauling his sister, he slipped his hand in the crook of her elbow and began hurrying her away. Abida resisted, struggling to free herself. Seeing the struggle, the men on the roof began shouting insults at Ashraf, who tightened his grip on Abida's arm and hustled her along. Colleen, trotting to catch up, gasped, 'What the heck's up, Ash? It's only a bit of fun, for heaven's sake. Let go of her.'

'Mind your own business,' spat Ashraf, 'and don't call me Ash.'

'But you're hurting her,' protested Colleen, 'and she didn't do anything. It's not her fault that those guys –'

'Look.' Ashraf halted, jerking Abida to a stop. 'If you want to encourage a bunch of brain-dead cradle-

snatchers, that's your affair, but I won't have you corrupting my sister, so stay away from her. Just stay away,
that's all.'

'Corrupting . . . ?' Colleen's sense of outrage
rendered her speechless. She stood quivering as Ashraf
turned his back on her and hurried his sister away. She
watched them recede, spitting and snarling at each
other. The men on the roof had lost interest. A fresh
avalanche of slates crashed into the truck. Colleen
moved on.

SIXTEEN

'He said *what*?'

'I won't have you corrupting my sister.'

'Huh!' cried Stephen. 'What a flipping cheek! Wait
till I get hold of him.'

'No.' Colleen shook her head. It was breaktime.
Brother and sister were talking near the bike sheds.
'Just leave it, Steve. Abi's my friend. I don't want
trouble between you and Ash.'

'No, but –'

'Leave it, OK? He probably didn't mean anything
by it.'

Stephen didn't argue but when classes resumed he

kept glancing at Ashraf, trying to decide whether to say something at hometime. He didn't want to spoil Colleen and Abida's friendship, but you can't let someone insult your sister, can you?

Funny guy though, old Ash, thought Stephen. Funny guy lately. Giving me a hard time over that kid getting mugged, as if it was my fault. And now having a go at Colleen.

Mind you, he's not the only one. What about those three guys at The Valley? *Want to make something of it?* Talk about touchy. Well – I didn't say anything 'cause there were three of them, but there's only one Ash.

Asians, though. They've all been Asians. It's as if Asian lads have suddenly decided to get stroppy. Makes you wonder whether they've been got at by those whatsits – fundamentalists. Yeah – maybe that's it.

And then that other guy. The heavy guy at The Valley. Our ground. Our town. Our country. *He's a fundamentalist all right. Don't matter where he's born, a Paki's a Paki.*

Wonder if *that's* what Blackout's on about though – fundamentalists? If so, maybe they've got a point. Maybe I'll give 'em a bell.

Yeah, maybe I will.

SEVENTEEN

'You are through to Blackout HQ. We're sorry – there's nobody in the office at the moment to take your call, but if you leave your name and number after the tone somebody will get back to you.'

'Great,' muttered Stephen. After the long beep he said, 'Steve Crowley on Shadderton six four six four seven eight. Thanks.' He hung up and went through to the kitchen. His mother was at the sink, washing lettuce. 'What's for tea, Mum?'

'Pizzas, baked potatoes and salad. Who were you calling, dear?'

'Nobody. Just making an inquiry but there was nobody there. Did Colleen tell you what Ash said to her this morning?'

His mother dumped a double handful of lettuce in a colander and shook her head. 'No. What *did* he say?'

'Only told her to stop corrupting his sister.'

'What on earth did he mean by that, Stephen?'

Stephen shrugged. 'Some demolition guys whistled at Col and Abi. Col waved back just as Ash came along so he's decided she's a slag.'

'Has he now?' She put the colander on the drainer

and began slicing tomatoes. 'The Khans are Muslims of course, and Muslims can be funny about – you know – their women. There was a piece in the *Post* the other day about that Imam – what's his name – Salaam, is it? The one who supports the Rushdie fatwa and wants separate schools for Muslim girls. Anyway, it seems he preached a sermon in which he said all English girls are loose and every English boy is a potential seducer.' She smiled. 'Perhaps your friend Ash has been listening to *him*.'

When the phone rang in the middle of tea, Stephen jumped up. 'That'll be for me.' He felt his cheeks burn as he went out into the hallway and picked up. 'Shadderton six four six four seven eight,' he said in a low voice. 'Steve Crowley speaking.'

'Oh hi, Steve. Thanks for leaving your number. Sorry there was nobody here. My name's Lawson, by the way. Martin Lawson. May I ask how you heard about us?'

'Sure. There was this guy at the match, Saturday. Broad guy. Leather jacket. Don't know his name. He gave me a leaflet.'

'Ah, right, that'd be Brian. Big United fan, our Brian. Fan yourself are you, Steve?'

'Since I was a kid.'

'An Ointment man, then?'

'Oh, no.' The Ointment were United's headbangers. 'I go for the game, not the aggro.'

'Against violence are you, Steve?'

'Well . . . yes. I mean, I'll fight if it can't be avoided

38

– I can look after myself, but I don't fight for fun if you know what I mean.'

'Oh, I know, I know.' The man chuckled. 'No point getting your head kicked in for no reason, but you'd fight for a cause. Am I right?'

'Yes.'

'Good. Have you had any . . . er . . . aggravation from our little tinted friends, Steve?'

'Sorry, who?'

'Non-whites, lad. Asians. Afros. Our little tinted friends.'

'No. Well . . . not really. Not directly. Just . . .'

'Verbal? Taunts and insults, that sort of thing?'

'Yes.'

'Yes, that's what we're finding. More and more of our people coming in for taunts and insults from these fellows who shouldn't be here in the first place. Look Steve, you sound like the sort of bright lad we at Blackout're always looking for. Why don't you come along to one of our meetings? D'you know the Waggon and Horses?'

'The pub on North Street?'

'That's the one. We've got the upstairs room there, Fridays, eight o'clock. You could pop along – no obligation – just sit in and see what you think.'

'But I'm only seventeen, Mr . . .'

'Martin. Call me Martin.'

'I'm only seventeen, Martin. Will I get in, with it being a pub I mean?'

'No problem, son. Lots of our members are seventeen. You don't even have to go through the bar. The stairs're on your right as you go in the doorway. Just walk up and you'll see the room. I look forward to meeting you, Steve. Thanks again for calling us. Bye.'

'Oh, but . . . OK. Bye.' Stephen stood for a moment, staring at the dead handset in his fist then shrugged, hung up and rejoined his family at the table.

EIGHTEEN

'No, leave that for a minute, please.' The evening meal was over and Zainab Khan had risen to clear the table. She sank back into her seat and looked at her husband. Ashraf and Abida gazed at him too.

'This letter came by the morning post.' Hassan unfolded the single sheet and smoothed it out. 'It is from the Housing Department. We are offered a three-bedroom flat on the Brockbank estate.'

'*Brockbank?*' cried Abida, aghast. 'Brockbank's the roughest estate in Shadderton, Dad. We can't live there.'

Her father shrugged. 'It's what they're offering, Abida. I don't see that we've a choice, and anyway it's only till the new shops are ready.'

'But the new shops won't be ready for over a year and a half,' put in Zainab. In deference to her, the conversation was in Urdu. Her husband smiled. 'A year and a half is not an eternity, my dear. It will pass, then we'll have a brand new unit with living accommodation. There'll be open space all round, and trees. Far better than Alma Street.

Ashraf shook his head. 'Space and trees're no use without customers, Dad, and you know it. This development, *if* it is ever completed, will scatter our people all over town.'

Hassan gazed at his son. 'I think you have been listening to your cousin Waseem.' He frowned. 'Why do you say, *if* it is ever completed, Ashraf? Of course it will be completed. The council is committed to it.'

Ashraf smiled. 'Doctor Lydgate was committed to ethical medicine till pressures diverted him from his intention.'

'Doctor Lydgate? Who is he, please?'

'A character in *Middlemarch*, Dad. What I'm saying is, there's going to be pressure on the council. Organized pressure. If it succeeds – if we act with determination and without fear – the Bennett Qureshi Millennium Development will never be finished.'

'*We*?' growled Hassan. 'Who is this we? I hope you're not telling me that you are involving yourself in this nonsense of Waseem's, Ashraf. This Khalifa?'

Ashraf nodded. 'Yes, Dad, I am. I am a member of

Khalifa, and someday our people will thank us for what we are about to do. *You* will thank us.'

Hassan looked his son in the eye. 'I will thank you, while you live under my roof and eat at my table, to attend to your studies and keep a respectful tongue in your head. Involve yourself in wrongdoing and I will throw you on to the street to fend for yourself. Do you understand?'

Ashraf nodded. 'I understand, but I have taken a vow and nothing can deflect me from my purpose. Nothing.'

Hassan looked at him. 'Wasn't that Doctor Lydgate's position, son?' he asked, mildly. 'Before the pressure, I mean?'

NINETEEN

Stephen reached the Waggon and Horses at five to eight Friday evening and everything was as Martin Lawson had said it would be. The street door stood open and the stairs were immediately inside on the right. He hesitated at the bottom, wondering what he might be getting himself into. He'd told his parents he was going to Bradley's house to do English homework. He'd even carried his backpack to make it look authentic. Perhaps it'd be better if he *did* go to Bradley's. That guy at the match, Saturday. Brian. He'd looked hard, and Martin had mentioned fighting for a cause. There could be a whole lot of trouble waiting at the top of these stairs.

He'd said no obligation though, hadn't he? Martin. No obligation. Just sit in and see what you think. Well OK then – I'll go for it.

As he reached the top, two men blocked his way. Big men with para cuts and biker jackets and lots of chunky gold jewellery. 'Where d'you think *you're* going, kid?' growled one.

'I . . . the meeting. Martin . . . Mr Lawson. He invited me.'

'Oh – *know* Mr Lawson, do you?'

'Yes. Well no, I don't know him. We spoke on the phone. After this guy called Brian gave me a leaflet at The Valley.'

'Ah-ha.' The man indicated Stephen's backpack. 'What's in there?'

'Nothing. School stuff. Just school stuff.'

'It's not a flaming *school* we're running here, kid.'

'I know.'

'So why bring school stuff?'

'To make my mum and dad think I'm doing homework at my mate's place.'

'Good God!' The man glanced at his companion. 'Hear that, Phil? Homework.'

The other man nodded. 'I heard, Dean. Makes you want to weep, dunnit?'

'All right.' The first man stepped aside and jerked

his head towards an open door. 'In there.' He sighed and shook his head as Stephen walked on. 'Be running a flaming *baby* clinic next, I shouldn't wonder.'

Stephen sat by himself on the back row. There were eighteen people in the room, not counting himself and two who sat behind a table out front, facing the rest. One of these was a man of about thirty who he guessed might be Martin Lawson. The other was eighteen or so, the only woman in the place. Most of those present had stared at him when he'd come through the door, and he was uncomfortably aware that two or three were watching him now, having twisted round in their seats to do so. He avoided eye contact, dumping his backpack on the dusty wooden floor then pretending to read the leaflet he'd brought with him. After a minute, the pair who'd stopped him outside came in and closed the door. The meeting began.

TWENTY

'In nineteen-oh-one, this country celebrated the start of a new century.' Martin Lawson gazed at his audience, letting his eyes flick from face to face. When they lighted on Stephen he gave a barely perceptible nod. Stephen nodded back, happy that his presence had been

matters into their own hands. It's not too late, providing we act now. We *can* make Britain a country to be proud of, but not while it's a dumping ground for the world's rubbish. We *can* look forward with optimism to a shining new millennium, but not through schemes with names like the Bennett Qureshi Millennium Development: schemes that ram integration down everybody's throat whether they like it or not.'

The speaker sat down, nodding and smiling in acknowledgement of loud, prolonged applause. This time Stephen joined in, clapping till his palms burned, thinking, he's no mug, this Lawson. And it's not *racist*, the stuff he's saying about the state of the country, because it's *true*. Can't be racist if it's true, can it?

When the clapping petered out, Lawson stood up again and introduced the woman beside him. Her name was Wendy Shoesmith and she spoke of Shadderton Council's plan to rehouse hundreds of Asians on the Brockbank estate. It was, she said, a plot. A deliberate plot to force council tenants to accept black neighbours. As a result, whites waiting for council accommodation would be pushed to the bottom of the list. The fact was that the forces responsible for Britain's decline were using the millennium as an excuse to con the British people into accepting blacks as a permanent fixture, but they weren't going to get away with it. Not in Shadderton. Blackout, said Wendy, had a plan of action, the first phase of which would be put into operation next Monday evening, when she would address an emergency meeting of the Brockbank Residents' Association. Out of this would come an organization dedicated to overturning the council's plan, *if* everyone present tonight made it his business to be at that meeting. 'Together', she said, 'we can smash this plot, this communist plot of the council, but we must be strong. We must be united. We must be brave.'

The meeting broke up at nine o'clock. Stephen hoped Martin might speak to him but he clattered off downstairs to the bar with Wendy and some of the others. Brian, who had given him the leaflet, ignored him too, so he left the pub and sauntered through the dark, quiet streets, pondering all he'd seen and heard.

TWENTY-ONE

'Kader Motor Services. How may I help you?'
   'Oh, hello. May I speak to Waseem Kader, please?'
   'Who shall I say is calling?'
   'A friend. Tell him a friend wants a word.'
   'Hold the line please, sir, I'll see if he's available.'

'Hello?'
   'Waseem Kader?'
   'Yes. What can I do for you?'

'It's more a case of what I can do for you, Mr Kader. Have you heard of an organization calling itself Blackout?'

'I've heard of it, yes. What about it?'

'And have you also heard that the council plans to rehouse people on the Brockbank estate, including a lot of Asians?'

'Yes, it was in the paper. Can we get to the point please – I *am* at work, you know.'

'Yes, I'm sorry about that but I don't have your home number. I thought you should know that the Brockbank Residents' Association is due to meet on Monday evening, and that Blackout plans to be there in force. I fancy the idea is to whip up hostility against Asian tenants before they even move in.'

'And what does all this have to do with me, Mr . . . what *is* your name anyway?'

'Never mind my name. I thought Khalifa might want to do something about it.'

'Khalifa? Who's Khalifa? I don't know what you're talking about.'

'Oh, I think you do, Mr Kader. Anyway, the meeting's at seven thirty at the Brockbank Community Centre. Goodbye.'

'Hey, just a minute –'

'Mr Lawson?'

'Speaking.'

'Ah. You don't know me, Mr Lawson, but I must ask you to believe me when I say I have your best interest at heart. Yours, and Blackout's.'

'Who *is* this? What're you talking about?'

'Never mind, just listen. Do you know of an Asian outfit known as Khalifa?'

'No, I don't.'

'Well, it exists, I assure you. Right here in Shadderton, and it means to confront your people on Monday evening.'

'My people? I don't –'

'Yes you do. Brockbank Community Centre, seven thirty. Be prepared, as the Boy Scouts say. Goodbye.'

'Wait . . . oh, dammit!'

TWENTY-TWO

Four forty-five. Stephen picked up the remote, pointed it at the TV and clicked on BBC 1. Colleen looked up from the book she was reading. 'Do you *have* to?'

Her brother nodded. 'Gotta see how United got on, haven't I? It's only quarter of an hour.' Colleen sighed, stood up and left the room. Stephen sat down and watched the screen. Desmond Lyneham talked about rugby, then switched to the teleprinter. Some Scottish results came up. Dundee had drawn with Celtic, two apiece. Raith Rovers had beaten Motherwell one nil. A couple of non-league results came through and Lyneham broke in to say it was still goalless at Old Trafford. Stephen shook his head. 'I don't give a toss about Man U, Des. What about Shadderton?' Results were coming thick and fast now but the one that mattered did not appear, and soon it was time for the classified check. Stephen sat impatiently through the Premiership, and when Division One came up there was a letter L against the Bradford City/Shadderton United fixture. 'Late *kick*-off?' He couldn't believe it.

At the end of the check, Lyneham said, 'There was crowd trouble at the First Division match between Bradford City and Shadderton United. No details are available, but apparently the start of the second half was delayed. We hope to bring you the result of that match before the end of the programme.' Stephen waited, but the programme ended without further mention of the affair. He switched off and got up as his mother called him to his tea.

'Trouble at the United game,' he said, sitting down.

'Oh, yes?' His father glanced up. 'What sort of trouble?'

'Crowd. Second half was delayed. No details, no result. Bit of a bummer.'

'I hope nobody was hurt,' murmured his mother, pouring tea.

'He doesn't care about *that*,' said Colleen. 'All he's bothered about is his precious result.'

'No it's *not*,' retorted Stephen. 'I've got mates there. Bradley. Justin. Of course I care.'

'Perhaps they'll mention it on *Look North Saturday*,' said their mother.

Stephen nodded. 'Never thought of that. It'll be on if it's serious, and they'll give the result anyway.'

Tea over, the Crowleys went through to the living room. After brief summaries of other local results the newsreader said, 'Shadderton United's away game at Bradford City was marred by violence when a penalty awarded to the home-side on the stroke of half-time was saved by United goalkeeper, Webley. Webley was adjudged to have moved before the ball was struck and the referee ordered the penalty retaken. As City striker McCall put the ball in the back of the net, a number of Shadderton supporters ran on to the pitch and tried to reach the referee. They were prevented from doing so by police, but Bradford fans joined in and fighting broke out. The referee took both teams off the field, dogs were brought in to control the rampaging fans and the start of the second half was delayed by ten minutes. Two people were taken to hospital where their injuries were found to be superficial. Bradford City won the match by two goals to nil.'

'Two nil,' groaned Stephen. 'First away match of the season and they go down two nil.'

'Nobody was seriously hurt though,' said his mother. 'That's the main thing.'

'They're lunatics, those fans,' growled her husband. 'They want locking up.'

'*All* soccer fans are lunatics,' murmured Colleen.

'Yeah, like all white girls are slags,' rejoined her brother.

'That'll do, you two,' rapped their father. 'There's enough trouble in the world without families falling out.' As he spoke, the phone rang. Colleen, expecting a call, went into the hallway and picked up. Stephen was passing her on his way upstairs when she turned and held out the handset. 'It's for you,' she said. 'Martin somebody.'

TWENTY-THREE

'Are you with us this morning, Ashraf Khan?'

'Y-yessir.'

'Then stop daydreaming, lad, and answer the question.'

'Question, sir?' He'd been thinking about tonight. About Khalifa. He'd heard no question.

'Q-U-E-S-T-I-O-N. You *are* familiar with the word, I take it? You do understand English?'

The familiar slur provoked a stab of anger in Ashraf. His self-respect cried out for some fierce response but common sense prevailed. 'I was born in England,' he said quietly, leaving out the sir. It would have to do. For now.

'The question, you sad pleb, is this. What did we decide last Thursday about the marriages of Casaubon and Lydgate?'

'We said . . . I think we decided that Casaubon wanted a secretary and Lydgate wanted an ornament. Sir.'

'That is correct, Ashraf. Thank you. It seems you *didn't* sleep through the entire session after all, and that gratifies me.' He sighed. 'The zoologists tell us the dormouse is the only terrestrial mammal in Britain which hibernates but this is inaccurate, as they would know if they'd ever tried teaching A level English in late summer.'

The class tittered. Ashraf shrugged and gazed stolidly at his copy of *Middlemarch*. Across the room sat Stephen, his lower lip caught between his teeth. His mind was on Brockbank where, unbeknown as yet to either of them, he and Ashraf would meet tonight, not as classmates but as enemies.

TWENTY-FOUR

Six o'clock, Monday evening. Stephen sat on the edge of his bed, gazing out over tired September gardens. It was decision time and he was torn.

I don't have to go, he thought. I don't have to be at the Waggon and Horses at seven, just 'cause Martin Lawson phoned. It was a crafty call, that. Left no room for refusal. For choice. *Crunch time, Steve*, Lawson had said in that crisp, no-nonsense voice of his. *Time to fight for that cause*. Well OK, I *did* say I'd fight for a cause but I didn't know it'd be so soon, and anyway I never said I'd fight for *their* cause. I don't even believe in Blackout. They're racist and I'm not. I only went to the meeting out of curiosity, to see what it was like, and they ignored me. Went off down to the bar without so much as a glance in my direction. So. I'm not a member, right? I don't owe them. I can sit and read *Middlemarch* or watch telly and let 'em get on with it.

They'll think I'm chicken though, won't they? What was it that big daft plonker said – *be running a flaming baby clinic next*. Yeah, they'll think I'm chicken all right.

So what do I care? Let 'em think what they like.

I'm not getting myself smashed up just to prove I'm not scared.

Mind you, it'd be a chance to make up for that fiasco at The Valley last week when I had to take it because there were three of them and only one of me. They might even be *there*, and I wouldn't be by myself this time. I can just see the looks on their faces. That'd be absolutely brilliant.

Yeah!

TWENTY-FIVE

'Is this Jennifer Most?'

'Yes. Who am I speaking to?'

'Never mind. I'm calling to put you in the way of a scoop.'

'A scoop?' The columnist sighed inaudibly. She'd had a long day. 'What sort of scoop, Mr . . . ?'

'Listen. There's a meeting at the Brockbank Community Centre at seven thirty. There's going to be trouble. Racial violence.'

'How do you know this?'

'I just do. Be there – you won't be disappointed.'

'I can't just . . . I need to know your name.'

'No name.'

'All right, but why are you calling me rather than the police? They could be there before anything started, nip it in the bud.'

'Ah, but you see, I don't *want* it nipped in the bud, Miss Most. Some of us are all for a bit of the old racial tension.' He chuckled. 'And so are you, I should think. Sells papers.'

'The *Post* is more concerned with promoting harmony than with selling papers, Mr . . . whoever you are. *I'll* call the police.'

'Suit yourself. You want to throw away a sensational front-page story, that's your funeral. Bye.'

Jennifer Most hung up and stood for a moment, uncertain how to proceed. She'd said she'd call the police, but what could she tell them? '*A guy says there's trouble brewing at Brockbank. Racial trouble. No, he wouldn't give his name. No, I don't know who's involved.*' Would they take any notice, send a car? she wondered. They'd want *my* name, and if nothing happens – if my caller's some nutcase . . .

No. What I'll do is drive over there, park where I can watch. If anything looks like starting I'll call them up on the mobile, and if it doesn't . . . well, nobody's any the wiser, right?

Right.

TWENTY-SIX

When Ashraf got to the rec, Waseem was there already, leaning on a goalpost. He shot his cuff to look at his watch. 'Ten-past. I said seven.'

The younger boy nodded. 'I know. I'm sorry. I had to mind the shop while Mum did something or other upstairs.' He peered at his cousin, who seemed to be hiding something under his jacket. 'What you got there?'

'This.' Waseem opened the garment, then closed it again. Ashraf swallowed.

'Baseball bat . . . you think it'll be *that* rough?'

'You kidding? With Blackout? *Course* it'll be that rough, or rougher. Why?' He gazed at Ashraf. 'Aren't you up for it?'

'Sure I am. Wouldn't be here, would I? I'm not carrying anything though.'

''S OK. Your boots'll do. Come on.'

Ten minutes of brisk walking brought them to the fringe of the Brockbank estate. The community centre was visible a hundred metres up the road. Waseem laid a hand on his cousin's arm. 'Hang on. I want to make sure some of the others're here before we go barging in.' Cars lined the kerb outside the centre. As they watched, others arrived, parking both sides of the road. People climbed out. Some went towards the building, others hung around their vehicles. After a minute, a gold Mondeo cruised by. Waseem nodded after it. 'Basir Khan. It's OK now.'

They advanced. The Mondeo had parked. Four men got out and leaned on the car, gazing across its roof at a cluster of whites round a Suzuki. The whites stared back. To reach the Mondeo, Ash and Waseem had to pass the Suzuki. As they did so, one of the men called after them. 'Hey Pakis – go home! No good here. Plenty bovver soon. You no go, you flatten like chapatti.' His companions guffawed. Ashraf glanced sidelong at Waseem, hoping his cousin couldn't see how scared he was.

They joined the group round the Mondeo. Ashraf recognized the middle-aged man who had conducted Monday's meeting. Karim Majid was also there. They greeted the newcomers with nods. Nobody smiled.

'I make it six of us, nine of them,' murmured the middle-aged man, whom Ashraf guessed was Basir Khan. He didn't once take his eyes off the whites as he spoke. 'Not ideal, but if their speaker shows up before any more of our lot, we'll have to make our move. Once they're inside the building it'll be too late.'

As he spoke, a white Honda parked. Two people got out, one of them a woman. 'That's her,' hissed Khan. 'Come on.'

The six whites had already detached themselves from the Suzuki and were crossing the road. Three more were approaching from the right. Ignoring all of these, Basir Khan strode to intercept the speaker and her escort. The others followed him. He caught the woman's sleeve as she reached the doorstep. 'Madam, why do you want to make trouble for those who are coming to live –'

'GERROFF!' The man with Wendy Shoesmith grabbed Basir Khan by the scruff of the neck and went to ram his face against a doorpost. Before he could do so, the others fell on him. They were wrestling him to the ground, kicked and pummelled by the enraged woman, when the nine closed in. Ashraf had time to see Waseem raise his bat before a terrific blow on the shoulder knocked him sideways. He fell on one knee, looking up into the wild eyes of the chain-wielding youth who had felled him. The chain, its heavy links red with rust, was descending again, and when he tried to throw up his arms to shield his head the left arm wouldn't move. Desperately he flung himself to one side. The chain whistled past his face and thudded against his shin, making him scream with pain. His left shoulder felt as though it was on fire. He sprawled helpless on the grass as the chain rose once more against the evening sky. This is it, he thought. This one smashes my skull. He screwed up his eyes.

There was no third blow. Somewhere a siren was

59

howling. All around men were shouting, skidding on turf, running. He heard the word 'police'. Thankfulness washed over him, but only for an instant. He thought of his father picking up the phone, learning that his son was under arrest. The siren was louder now. It was close. Very close. He started to get up, glancing about him for Waseem. 'Waseem!' he gasped. 'Where are you? I can't . . .'

He was on his feet, left arm dangling. Everything hurt. He felt like throwing up but he swallowed instead and started to run. A figure loomed in front of him. Shiny buttons. He swerved. More shiny buttons. Somebody grabbed his arm. His bad arm. Pain like he'd never known. Unbelievable. Flatten like chapatti, he thought. Everything went black.

TWENTY-SEVEN

'Somebody always calls the police.' Martin Lawson had issued this warning to his followers in the Waggon and Horses car park. 'Somebody always calls the police, so whatever else you're doing, listen out for that siren and when you hear it, scarper. If the other fella gets arrested, so much the better for us. Gives his organization a bad name.'

Well, thought Stephen, crouching behind a row of wheelie bins at the kitchen end of Brockbank First School. Lawson was right. Somebody *did* call the police and I *did* scarper and here I am, a bit out of breath but otherwise OK. I'll wait a bit longer to make sure, but I doubt if anyone'll come now.

For Stephen, the clash had been fairly mild. He'd been scared, sitting in the car beside the guy with the chain hanging out of his pocket. He'd been scared when it was time to move in and protect Wendy from Khalifa, but they were fighting in lumps by the time he arrived. All he'd done was dance round the ruck, lashing out with feet or fists whenever a target presented itself. Nobody had hit him, and because he was on the fringe he'd been one of the first away when the law showed up.

The worst bit had been seeing Ash. Stephen hadn't spotted him till the mêlée broke up and there he was, lying on the grass. He'd nearly stopped to help him up, remembering just in time that his fallen friend represented the enemy. Ash, though. A member of Khalifa. It was hard to believe. Mind you ... He chuckled, shaking his head. What about me, a member of Blackout?

I'm not a member, he thought. One meeting, that's all. Two if you count this. I shan't go again. Kicking guys from behind. Running from the law. Hiding behind wheelie bins. Not my style.

He looked at his watch. Twenty to eight. Wendy'll

be speaking now. I wonder . . . I wonder if I dare stroll back there, dead cool, join the meeting. I look OK don't I? Not like a guy who's been in a fight. Just a respectable citizen arriving a bit late for a meeting.

It's a daring thing to do though, right? Swashbuckling. Yeah, that's the word. Swashbuckling.

TWENTY-EIGHT

Wendy Shoesmith paused momentarily as the door at the back opened to admit a youth who tiptoed to a vacant chair in the back row. Then, with a glance at her notes, she continued.

'Did the council *ask* you if you wanted seventy Asian families on the Brockbank Estate? Was this association consulted in any way? No it was not, and why? Because when it comes to pushing through their unwanted racial policies, the ruling group finds the democratic process inconvenient. They know that if people were asked, the answer would be a resounding no, so they don't ask. They don't ask. They sneak it through, and before you know it you've got people next door playing the bongos all night and doing their business in the garden. *They* don't, of course. Your councillors. Oh no. No. *They* all live out in suburbia where everyone's white and the gardens are immaculate. You try shoving eighty Asian families out *there* and see how far you'd get.'

'Ah, but just a minute, love.' A man in the fourth row had his hand up. 'Aren't you confusing the issue? I mean, the council consists of elected members and we elected them, knowing their policy on integration. That's the same as being asked, surely? If you had to go round asking every individual on the —'

'Sir.' The association's chairman, who was sitting beside Wendy, interrupted. 'You *must* allow the speaker to proceed. There'll be time for questions at the end.'

'Yes but —'

'At the *end*, sir, please!'

'It's a fair point I'm making, Mr Chairman. It deserves —'

'Not now. Sit down or I'll have to ask you to leave.'

The noise level rose as people in the audience joined in on one side or the other. Cries of 'sit down' and 'shut up' were countered by demands to let the man speak. Wendy Shoesmith shuffled her notes, waiting for the hubbub to die. A man in front of Stephen got up and crabbed along the row, excusing himself as he pushed past knees and stepped on toes. Stephen recognized Brian Maxwell, the football fan. He watched as Brian walked down to the fourth row, bulldozed his way to the middle, plonked himself down on a vacant seat beside the man who had interrupted and leaned over to murmur in his ear. Stephen couldn't hear what Brian was saying, but whatever it was caused the man to stop waving at the platform and to sit very still. The chairman gestured to Wendy to continue, but he had a funny look on his face and Stephen could tell he was more than a little dubious about Blackout's method of keeping order.

TWENTY-NINE

Tuesday teatime. Michael Crowley was sipping his second cup and scanning the *Post*. 'Hmm. *Thought* there'd be trouble over that.'

His wife glanced up, scone half-buttered. 'Over what, dear?'

'Moving those families out to Brockbank. There was a fight last night outside the community centre.'

'Involving whom?'

'Doesn't really say. White and Asian youths. One Asian arrested.' He frowned. 'Ashraf Khan. Isn't he a friend of yours, Stephen? Abida's brother?'

Stephen practically choked on his scone. 'Y-yeah. Might be him. Common name though.'

His father shook his head. 'Ashraf Khan of 33 Alma Street. That's the shop. It's him all right. Daft young sod, getting involved. Police reckon he was armed with a heavy chain, too. I'd knock some sense into him if he was mine, I can tell you. Getting his name in the paper.'

'He thinks Colleen's corrupting his sister,' said Sonia, glancing at her daughter.

Colleen shook her head. 'Ash is a Muslim, Mum. He didn't mean anything. And he was probably fighting for his beliefs last night.'

'Hooo!' mocked Stephen. 'Note how she leaps to his defence, *then* tell me she hasn't got the –'

'Stephen!' His mother glared. 'We'll have no repetition of *that* vulgarity, thank you very much. And beliefs are no excuse for brawling in the street, Colleen. I think you'd both better stay away from Ashraf Khan if that's the sort of lad he's turning out to be.'

'Your mother's right,' growled Michael. 'We don't want *our* name all over the front page.' He looked up. 'Pass the milk, please, Colleen.'

The meal resumed in silence, for which Stephen was thankful. He'd half expected his dad to start quizzing him about his whereabouts last night, which would have been embarrassing, plus he needed time to think about Ash. A heavy chain. Armed with a heavy chain, the paper says, but he had no weapon when I saw him. I know who *did* have a chain. The guy I sat beside in the car. I wonder . . .

At ten to eleven that night, Colleen knocked and came into her brother's room with a funny expression on her face. 'What's up?' growled Stephen. 'You've a face on you like a slapped arse.'

'Abida phoned. She says you were there last night.'

'Where?'

'You know. Brockbank. You were one of the white youths.'

'Was I heck. How would *she* know?'

'Ash told her. He saw you. He . . . needs your help.'

'I wasn't there I tell you. What help?'

'It's about the weapon he's supposed to have been carrying. The chain. It was found near him but it wasn't his. He says you know that.'

'*How* do I know? I wasn't even there.'

'Oh yes you were, Steve. I always know when you're lying.' She shook her head. 'You needn't worry, I won't tell, only you've got to help Ash. That chain makes the charge really serious. He could go to prison. You will tell what you know, won't you?'

Stephen shook his head. 'I dunno. It's not that easy, is it? I mean, suppose I do come forward. They won't let me do it in secret, will they? Dad'll find out, then what?'

Colleen shrugged. 'I don't know, Steve, but you won't end up in jail, will you? Not like Ash.'

'I might. The police'd know I was involved. What's to stop 'em arresting me?'

'OK, they might arrest you. They might, but you've still got to tell. You can't just let Ash –'

'Let me think about it, Col, OK? It's more compli-

cated than you know. There's another guy involved.'
He laughed briefly. 'I could wind up dead.'

'What d'you mean, dead? Is that a joke or what? Dead?
What . . . what are you mixed up in, Steve? Who's –'

'I told you, Col, just leave it. I've got to think.'

'OK.' His sister moved towards the door. 'Only
don't take too long. Ash's trial's in two weeks. You're
his only chance.'

THIRTY

A pall of gloom shrouded the Khan household. Ashraf,
out on bail, was confined to his room, his collarbone
fractured by the first blow from the chain the police
were saying was his. His left arm was in a sling and he
hadn't been to school that day. Abida had, but under
strict instructions from her father to talk to nobody
about her brother's arrest. She'd wanted to confide in
Colleen but had avoided her instead, lurking in the
cloakroom at break, hurrying off the instant school was
over. In the early evening, with both parents in the
shop, she'd been able to talk briefly with her brother
through his door. He'd told her he'd seen Stephen
Crowley during last night's mêlée and that Stephen
knew the owner of the chain. Her father, coming

through from the shop at an unfortunate moment, had caught her on the phone and overheard part of her conversation with Colleen. He was furious.

'Did I hear you say your friend's brother was involved in the fight last night?'

'Yes, Dad. Ashraf saw him.'

'So why did the police arrest my son and not him?'

'I don't know. Ash was hurt. Couldn't get away. I expect Stephen ran.'

'No doubt. And what were you saying about the chain?'

'Ash says Stephen knows who had the chain. It was one of the white men. I've asked Colleen to speak to her brother – persuade him to tell the police.'

'And?'

Abida shrugged. 'She says she'll ask him.'

'He will not tell, Abida. It would be admitting he was there. It was wrong of you to make the call.'

'I was trying to help Ash, Dad. He could go to prison.'

'He should have thought of that before he involved himself in violence. I warned him.'

'He went because Waseem asked him,' defended Abida. 'He looks up to his cousin. Always has.'

Her father nodded. 'I know. Waseem shares the blame but Ashraf is not a child. He has a mind of his own. He chose to be at the scene and must face the consequences. Still . . .' Hassan slammed his right fist into his left palm. 'It isn't fair that he should be the only one. Why were none of the whites arrested, that's what I'd like to know.'

Abida shook her head. 'I don't know, Dad, but I know this. By asking that question you are playing into the hands of the violent. They *want* to sow distrust in our hearts. Distrust of the authorities. The law.'

Her father nodded grimly. 'Yes, well, if that's what they want I'm afraid they've got it. The police themselves say there were at least fifteen people outside that community centre. With the best will in the world I can't believe they couldn't have caught more than one.'

Abida sighed. 'I'm sure they did their best, Dad.'

'You are a child, Abida. You know nothing. Go through to the shop, please. Help your mother. I will speak with my son.'

THIRTY-ONE

'Why assembly?' hissed Tracey Wigmore as Year Twelve filed into the hall. 'It's only Wednesday.'

Justin Case grinned. 'The staff syndicate's won the lottery. They're throwing a party for us this morning and jetting off to California straight after.'

'You wish,' muttered Tim O'Brien as the class filled its slot at the back. Mr Greenglass cleared his throat.

'Settle down, Year Twelve. This is assembly, not a rave.'

The Head, Mr Pelham, strode on to the platform and stood, holding the lapels of his hairy jacket like the headmaster in an Edwardian school photograph, gazing down. When every eye in the hall was on him, he spoke. 'No doubt some of you are wondering why we are assembled here on a Wednesday morning when we ought to be in our classes.'

'No,' breathed Justin Case. 'We're not wondering at all. In fact we don't give a toss.'

'I have called you together to speak on a matter of some gravity.'

'Oh, *gravity*,' mumbled Justin. 'Isaac Newton and that. Apples falling. Right.'

'I know that many of you will have read the piece in yesterday's *Post* about the regrettable incident outside the community centre on the Brockbank estate, involving among others a boy from this school.' He paused, his eyes sweeping the rows of upturned faces. 'It seems that Shadderton is not to escape the scourge of racial intolerance which from time to time plagues our towns and cities, but I tell you this. Here at Shadderton Comprehensive there will be no such scourge. Our school is a community. *One* community. There is no intolerance here. No division according to race, creed or colour. Never has been and never will be, because I for one will not tolerate it.'

'But, sir, that's intolerance,' whispered Justin. Giggles broke out around him. The Head's eyes sought the source of the disturbance and locked in. 'Evidently some pupils in Year Twelve find this topic amusing. Case, Wigmore, O'Brien. Hold on to that sense of humour, you three. You'll need it when you report to my office at three fifteen.' His eyes moved away as he continued. 'As I was saying, there's to be no nonsense of this sort at school. Any racial abuse, physical or verbal, will be severely punished. We are all sisters and brothers here and we will conduct ourselves accord-ingly.' He scanned the faces once more. 'I trust I have made myself quite clear. Stephen Crowley?'

'S-sir?'

'Step along to my office in five minutes, please.'

THIRTY-TWO

The sign on Pelham's door read: T. PELHAM B. Ed. HEAD TEACHER. Stephen hesitated, ner-vous as a Year Nine. What the heck does he want me for? He inhaled deeply and knocked.

'Come.' Come. Thinks he's a flipping Mogul emperor.

'You wanted to see me, sir?'

'Ah yes, Stephen.' Pelham was in his swivel chair. There was a chair this side of the desk too but he didn't invite Stephen to sit. 'A girl from Year Ten came to see me before assembly, Stephen. Abida Khan.'

'Sir?'

The Head gazed at him. 'You know what she came about, I take it?'

'No, sir.'

'Oh. I felt sure you would. Her brother's a friend of yours, isn't he?'

'Well . . . sort of, sir.'

'Sort of. I see. Well anyway, Ashraf's got himself into a spot of bother with the police. I assume you know this, and Abida tells me you are in possession of information which could help the lad. Is this correct?'

Stephen didn't answer at once. He couldn't. Fury blazed in him as the truth dawned. That Abida. Last night she talked Colleen into trying to persuade me to tell what I know, even though by doing so I could get myself into serious trouble. And I didn't say no. I could have, but I didn't. I said I'd think about it and Colleen'll have told Abida this on the walk to school, so why . . . why come blabbing to the Head? Why put me on the spot like this instead of giving me time?

'Well, Stephen? *Is* this correct, or isn't it? Do you have information? If you have, it's your duty to come forward.'

Stephen inhaled deeply, controlling his anger. Controlling, not dispersing. You blew it, Abi. Nobody drops me in the shit. He looked straight in Pelham's eyes and shook his head.

'The girl's mistaken, sir. I have no information. I wasn't even there.'

THIRTY-THREE

'Mr Lawson?'

'Yes.'

'I phoned last Saturday to warn about Khalifa. Your people handled the situation quite well on the whole, I thought. One of theirs arrested, and they failed to nobble your speaker. Excellent. I believe it's time you and I met.'

'Who are you? What's your interest in all this?'

'All in good time, Mr Lawson. Tell me, could your organization use some funding – say ten thousand pounds?'

'Ten thou –'

'For a start. Ten thousand for a start. It'd help you fight the Bennett Qureshi Millennium Development, wouldn't it?'

'Help? It'd make victory absolutely certain, Mr . . . ?'

'I thought it might. Do you know the roadhouse

on the left, halfway between Shadderton and Newmill?
The Golden Goose?'

'I know it.'

'Tomorrow evening, eight thirty, lounge bar. Come alone.'

'How . . . how will I know you?'

'I'll know *you*, Mr Lawson. Eight thirty, then. Goodbye.'

THIRTY-FOUR

'Steve!' Colleen called to her brother as he overtook, walking with his head down. He turned, shot a hostile glance at Abida and looked at his sister. 'What?'

'Have you . . . did Pel talk to you, about Ash?'

'Yes he did. He sent for me because *she* went and blabbed, told him I was there.' He glared at Abida. 'What d'you want to go and do that for, eh? Don't you know I could be arrested? Chucked in jail? Didn't Colleen tell you I was thinking about it?'

Abida nodded. 'Yes, Stephen, she told me, but I . . . I'm so worried about my brother. So worried. I wanted to make sure you'd make the right decision, and quickly.'

'And you thought grassing me up'd do it for you?

You're barmy, Abida. It was the worst thing you could do. The worst. You blew it, in fact. I *was* thinking about it. I'm not any more.'

Colleen gazed at him. 'You mean you're not going to do it? You're going to let –?'

'I'm going to *let* nothing, Col. It's got sod all to do with me, because I wasn't there.'

'You *were*. Of course you were, else why would you agree to think about it?'

'You can't prove I agreed. There were no witnesses. It's your word against mine.'

'I can tell Dad you were involved.'

'Yes, but there again there's no proof. I'll deny it, that's all.' He looked at Abida. 'You should've kept your mouth shut, kid. Now it's too late. See you.' He spun on his heel and walked away.

THIRTY-FIVE

Colleen didn't split on her brother but she didn't go out of her way to be nice to him either. Stephen, tired of hassle, trod softly for a couple of days, working his way into *Middlemarch* and being polite to his parents. He'd virtually decided he preferred the quiet life when Martin Lawson phoned.

It was Friday teatime. Michael, hanging his jacket in the hallway, picked up. The caller asked if Stephen was there. 'Who shall I say is calling?' asked Michael. He called out, 'Stephen – for you. Somebody Lawson.' Stephen waited till his father left the hallway then mumbled his name into the mouthpiece. He wished Lawson hadn't called. It could only be about tonight's meeting and he hadn't planned to go.

'Hello, Steve. Nice job, Monday. Brian tells me you went back to the meeting. Gutsy, that. I'm impressed.'

'Thanks.'

'No, I mean it. You're the sort of guy I like to have around. We'll see you tonight, I take it. Eight o'clock.'

'Well, as a matter of fact I –'

'Listen. I've got big news for tonight's meeting. Really big. I want everybody there. All the troops. Blackout's about to become a major force in this town and you can be part of it, Steve. A big part. I've got my eye on you.'

Lawson must have phoned everybody, because when Stephen got there at five to eight, the upper room at the Waggon and Horses was packed. Too late for a seat, he had to stand at the side in a pack of hot, jostling bodies. Lawson, behind his table out front, looked jubilant.

'Last night at this time,' he began, when the stragglers had shoved their way in and the doors were closed, 'I was at a pub a few miles from here, waiting to meet a certain gentleman.'

'Oh aye?' called a wag at the back. 'And we all thought you were a happily married man, Martin.' Laughter. Lawson smiled, waiting for quiet.

'I *am* happily married,' he resumed, 'but I left that meeting happier still.' He paused for dramatic effect. 'I'm not at liberty to talk about the gentleman except to say that he's a respected figure here in Shadderton, and that he's offered to fund our campaign against the B-Q-M-D to the tune of ten thousand pounds.'

Gasps of amazement were followed by a crescendo of cheers and whistles. Under cover of this, Stephen looked quizzically at the youth beside him. 'B-Q-M-D?'

'Bennett Qureshi Millennium Development,' growled the youth.

'Oh, right,' mumbled Stephen, feeling himself blush. Of *course*. What a plonker.

When the noise died down, Lawson revealed that ten thousand was just for starters, and went on to talk about the difference such funding would make to Blackout's ability to operate. He spoke of organizing the membership into a number of what he called commandos, each under its own leader. The commandos would operate independently, striking at targets identified by the leaders in conference, with himself as supremo and Brian Maxwell as deputy. Special training sessions would be set up, with outside experts being brought in to teach skills such as the construction of incendiary devices and timing mechanisms, disabling of motor vehicles, unarmed combat skills, resistance under interrogation and many more. It was heady stuff.

Walking home afterwards, Stephen fantasized himself in the role of commando leader, at seventeen taking his men into action with dash and flair. Well, he told himself, it's not all that far-fetched. What had Martin said on the phone? 'I've got my eye on you.' What did that mean, if not that he was being groomed for leadership? He shivered. Heady stuff, but a bit scary. A *lot* scary in fact. Still. He smiled to himself. Beats boredom, right?

THIRTY-SIX

The young reporter hung up the phone and yelled across the newsroom. 'Hey, Jenny, O.B.S. wants a word. Now. In his office.'

'Shit!' Jennifer Most snatched a sheet from the printer, balled it up and tossed it towards the waste-paper basket. It hit the rim, bounced out and rolled under the desk. 'Shit, shit, triple shit,' she hissed, shoving back the swivel chair. 'That's *all* I need on a Saturday morning – a barney with the boss.'

O. B. STOCKS read the nameplate on the door. MANAGING EDITOR. Jennifer knocked and entered. Stocks smiled at her across a cluttered desk the size of a soccer field. 'Have a seat, Jenny. Smoke?' He leaned forward, offering the silver box.

Jennifer shook her head. 'I don't.'

'Course you don't,' chuckled the editor. 'Old men forget.' He stuck a cigarette between his lips, lit up with a table lighter, drew deeply and instead of exhaling, spoke. Smoke puffed and curled out of his mouth with every syllable, veiling his face. 'That spot of bother last Monday night. Brockbank. Somebody told me you were there. That right?'

'Yes, that's right. I'd had a tip-off. Anonymous call.'

'Man or woman?'

'Man.'

'And you've no idea . . . ?'

'None. A scoop he called it, which I fancy makes him elderly.'

'Hmm. Never mind, that's not what I wanted to talk to you about. Thing is, Jenny, that unless I'm seriously mistaken, there's a nasty situation brewing. Racial thing. It's partly to do with this rehousing scheme of the council's of course, but I can't help feeling there's something else. Something bigger. Anyway, I've been mulling it over and I believe it's time the *Post* took a stand. A positive stand against intolerance and violence, and in favour of harmony.' He flicked ash into a brass tray. 'I want you to do a column.'

'A column?'

'Yes. A weekly column, Fridays, under your own byline. I thought, *Most in the Post.*'

'Most . . . ?' The woman frowned. 'What sort of column had you in mind, boss? I mean, what would it have to do with harmony?'

'I'm coming to that. I thought, a series of pieces about the lives of individual Shaddertonians. You know – their histories, their hopes and fears, their *feelings* about things. Let people see that we're all basically the same – we love our kids, our homes, our leisure. We want these things protected. All we ask – all we *really* want, whether our parents hail from Bombay or Bolton – is a quiet life. I thought it might be a good idea to start with one of the families they're shoving out to Brockbank. What d'you think?'

'Well, I . . . it's worth a shot, I suppose. When were you thinking of –?'

'First piece this coming Friday. Look.' He slid a printout through the debris. 'Here's the address of the Khan family. It's a shop. Their son's the guy the police arrested at the scene, Monday, but I don't want a piece about that. Tell us about *them*, as a family.' He gazed through blue smoke. 'Think you can hack it?'

Jennifer shrugged. 'Certainly, provided the Khans'll

talk to me at all. I mean, they're bound to be upset, their son under arrest and all that.'

The Managing Editor nodded. 'I don't expect it'll be easy, Jenny. Few things are in this life, but I've every confidence in you.' He twinkled. 'And you get a byline, remember. Ultimate accolade in our trade.'

'Yeah, right.' She stood up, scanned the printout and sighed. 'Alma Street here I come. Ready or not.'

THIRTY-SEVEN

Half the houses on Alma Street were abandoned already. Windows curtainless, doors ajar. Domestic jetsam littered the cracked flags. Polythene bags. Soggy magazines. A broken toy. Jennifer Most pulled over by the sad-looking corner shop, locked the mini and picked her way through the litter.

Zainab was behind the counter. 'Yes, please?'

Jennifer smiled. 'I'm Jennifer Most. I'm with the *Post*. I wonder if I might –'

Zainab frowned. 'Excuse me. You bring the post?'

'No, no. I'm with the *Post*. The newspaper. We'd like –'

'Wait one minute, please. I will get my husband.'

Zainab vanished through a bead curtain. Jennifer was gazing at a pyramid of tuna tins when the bell pinged and a boy of about sixteen came in. He looked at her. 'Is somebody seeing to you?'

'Oh yes, thanks.' He looked vaguely familiar. 'Do you live here?'

'Yes. My parents own the shop. Perhaps *I* can get you what you want?'

She shook her head. 'I'm not a customer, I'm from the paper. The *Post*. It's Ashraf, isn't it?'

'What do you want?' His tone was guarded. Hostile. 'If it's about Brockbank, we have nothing to say.'

She shook her head. 'It's not. Well – in a way it *is* I suppose, but not the fight.' That's where I saw you, she thought. At the fight. She smiled. 'We'd like to do a piece on the *move* to Brockbank – how it'll affect you as a family. How you feel about it.'

The boy scoffed. 'Doesn't matter how we feel, does it? It's all been decided. We've to be out by such-and-such a date and that's it.'

Jennifer nodded. 'Bureaucracy. I know. Decisions taken by faceless men behind closed doors, disrupting people's lives. We want to explore that. The cost to ordinary people in terms of plans frustrated. Shattered dreams.'

The youth's smile was tight. '"Destiny stands by sarcastic" and all that.'

'Pardon?'

'It's a quote. *Middlemarch*. Only it's not destiny, it's power. White power.'

'Oh, come *on*. That's exactly the sort of attitude that leads to trouble. It's what we hope to counter with our series.'

Ashraf shook his head. 'No chance. It's already started. You can't stop it. Nobody can. It's a fight against oppression. A fight for respect. Too long we've bowed down. Now we're going to –'

'Ashraf!' The boy broke off as his father came through the curtain. 'I told you, stay in your room. Talk to nobody. You've done too much damage already with your talk. Go.'

'I was only . . . this woman wants . . .'

'Go!' Hassan glared after his son as the boy strode round the end of the counter. The beads clashed as he swept through the curtain, which rippled for a time with the force of his going. Hassan turned to the woman. 'You must excuse my son. He has been keeping bad company and is under considerable strain.' He shrugged. 'We too are under strain. His mother and myself. Now – how may I help you?'

THIRTY-EIGHT

As Hassan Khan led Jennifer Most through the bead curtain, Abida left by the back door and walked towards the town centre. She was meeting Colleen at Carousel, the coffee shop in Shadderton's shopping mall. The two girls often did this on Saturdays – drinking Cokes, browsing the record and fashion shops and looking at any boys who might be around. Abida's parents weren't exactly crazy about her spending her time in this way and had sometimes told her so, but they'd never actually tried to stop her. A teenage kid who doesn't join in is going to wind up friendless and they didn't want that. Lately, Ashraf had become the biggest problem, urging her to break off her friendship with Colleen, stop speaking to Stephen and avoid white kids altogether, but she wasn't about to do any of these. It was a recipe for trouble and besides, why should she obey her brother, just because he was older and a boy?

Colleen had arrived at Carousel before her and got her a Coke. Abida slipped into the moulded plastic seat. 'Hi. Been here long?'

'Naw. Three minutes. Any hassle?'

'No. Ash is grounded.' She grinned. 'Makes things easier all round.'

Colleen pulled a face. 'Stephen's started now. "What d'you want to see *that* sneaky little so-and-so for?" he says, only he didn't say so-and-so. I'm not going to tell you what he *did* say.' She looked at her friend. 'I'm really sorry he won't help Ash, Abi.'

Abida nodded. 'I know. It's not your fault, Col. I just wish all this unpleasantness would go away. I've a feeling something's going to happen. Something nasty.'

Colleen sucked on her straw. 'Me too. Stephen's got himself mixed up with this . . . organization. Blackout. I saw a leaflet in his room. They sound a right lot of veg. I thought he'd more sense.'

'Same with Ash, only his lot call themselves Khalifa.'

'What's that mean?'

Abida shrugged. 'It's after some old-time hero or saint or something, in Islam. I think Ash sees himself as fighting a holy war. It's all so stupid.'

'I know. Anyway.' Colleen gazed at her friend. 'One thing we can do is promise it won't split us up. You and me, I mean.'

Abida nodded. 'Yes, we can do that.' She reached out, taking Colleen's hand. 'I promise.'

Colleen nodded. 'Me too. It's you and me, Abi. No matter what.'

THIRTY-NINE

The Nova turned on to Alma Street, cruising. Rehana, perched on her brother's knee in the front passenger seat, smiled. It was a good game, this. Karim's friend was driving. His name was Shazad. In the back sat two other men, watching her. She felt important, gazing out. A good game, with herself as captain.

'What about him?' asked Karim, as they passed a boy with a skateboard tucked under his arm. Rehana shook her head. The car moved on, turned a corner. 'These two?'

'No.'

'Him, then?'

'No.' She touched the scar on her chin, running a finger along its length. She knew that the game was linked in some way to her scar. It didn't hurt any more and most of the time she forgot it was there, but it bothered other people. Karim. These friends of his. Her father. It made them angry. They were angry now. Rehana could feel their anger and it excited her.

They were driving past the rec when she spotted them. They were with three other boys, kicking a ball around. 'There,' she squealed, pressing her face to the glass. 'That's them.'

The car pulled over. Karim put his head near hers, peering out. 'Which ones? The guy in goal?' The two in the back were leaning forward, waiting for her to speak. She nodded.

'Yes, and the one in the yellow shirt who just kicked the ball.'

'You sure, Rehana? It's important.'

'Yes.' She could hear him in her head, the one in goal. *You're a liar, same as all Pakis.* Well, this wasn't a lie. It was him all right.

'Can't do it here,' growled one of the men in the back.

'No.' Karim shook his head. The driver looked at him. 'So what do we do?'

'We wait.'

'Might as well save petrol then.' He switched off the engine and sat back. Karim hoisted Rehana from one knee to the other, fished in his pocket and produced a bag of jelly babies.

'There you go, kid – stop you getting bored.'

Rehana took the bag. 'Shuk ra.'

The driver wound down his window and lit a cigarette. People walked past. On the field the boys punted the ball around, shouting obscenities. Time passed.

Twelve noon. Karim shifted his sister, stretching his legs. The driver flicked a second butt out the window.

The men in the back talked softly. On the rec, a boy looked at his watch, called something to his friends and pulled his jacket from the pile they had for a goalpost. The game ceased. The owner picked up his ball. The boys retrieved their jackets, zipped them up and drifted off in various directions. Rehana's erstwhile attackers left the field together and strolled along Thornbury Road in muddy trainers, chatting. The driver started his engine and the Nova crept forward at three miles an hour. Rehana glanced in the vanity mirror and saw that the men in the back now had baseball bats across their knees. She shivered.

FORTY

They did it on a half-derelict street in the middle of the demolition area. It was so quick it was over before Rehana really knew what was happening. One minute the Nova was scrunching along twenty metres behind the two youths and the next it had shot forward and swerved on to the broken kerb in front of them, blocking their way. They saw instantly what was about to happen but it was too late. The rear doors flew open and out leaped two men wielding baseball bats. Unable to go forward or back, the boys attempted to dart across the road but one of the men got there first, cutting them off. The pair skidded to a stop, turned and ran into an empty house with the men at their heels. In the front passenger seat, Karim smiled. There'd be no need now to cover the child's eyes. What had to be done would be done out of sight. Things had worked out perfectly.

The men reappeared in thirty seconds, cradling their bats. They jogged to the car, slipped into their seats and slammed the doors. Nobody spoke. Shazad revved up and the Nova shot away. Karim smiled at Rehana. She was looking mystified but she'd done a great job. He tickled her ribs and she chuckled. Her breath smelled of raspberries.

FORTY-ONE

'Now then, Steve.' Brian Maxwell flopped down next to Stephen. It was two minutes to kick-off. The teams were punting balls around. A choir of home fans serenaded the visitors. 'You're in the Valley,' they sang. 'The Valley of death.'

Stephen smiled. 'Hi.'

'Have a look at this.' Maxwell pulled a polythene bag out of his biker jacket and dangled it. It contained a Stanley knife. Blood beaded the inside of the bag. Stephen pulled a face.

'Wh – what's that?'

Maxwell grinned wolfishly. 'Let's just say today's attendance is three down on what it should be.'

'Th – three down?'

'Yep. Your three mates from a fortnight ago, remember? They were in a bit of a rush to get through the turnstile.'

'I remember. You mean you've . . .' Stephen nodded towards the bag.

'One of 'em. The lippy one. His mates'll see him home, via the casualty department. I'd say seventeen stitches. Eighteen, possibly.' He shoved the bag back in his pocket.

Stephen felt nauseous. To cover up he said, 'I heard you got arrested at the Bradford game.'

The youth nodded. 'Managed to ditch the blade though. Two nights in a police cell and fined fifty quid Monday. Piece of cake. Listen. I've a message for you, from Martin.'

'What?'

'It's about Dean's chain. He slung it when the coppers showed up and they think one of the Pakis had it. Martin wants 'em to go on thinking that.'

'What's that got to do with me?'

'You were in the car with Dean. You saw the chain. And the Paki's in your class at school. Thing is, Martin'd be a bit peeved if you decided to chat to the law, and speaking for myself I'd hate to have to slice off one of your lugs, us both being United fans and all.'

A roar told Stephen the game had started. He looked at Maxwell. 'There was no need for Martin to send a message like that. I'd already decided to say nothing, and anyway I thought he trusted me.'

'Martin?' The youth laughed. 'Martin trusts nobody, kid. Anyway, you stick to your decision and you'll have something to hook your specs on when you're old. Now let's watch the game, eh?'

FORTY-TWO

'I don't know.' Michael Crowley folded the paper, slid it on to the coffee table and reached for the TV remote. 'Doom and flipping gloom, that's all they seem to print these days.'

His wife nodded. 'Violent crime all over the front page. You'd think they'd look for something cheerful to write about once in a while.'

'It's not their fault,' protested Colleen. 'If violent stuff happens, they've got to report it. It's their job.'

'Yes I know, but it's the way they seem to revel in

it that gets me. Great black headlines. I think it actually encourages people to be violent, giving it publicity like that.'

'Does it heck,' growled Stephen, who had just entered the room. 'Violent people act violently, that's all. They don't go through the papers looking for ideas. What's happened anyway?'

'Two horrible beatings,' sighed his mother. 'Both on Saturday. One poor lad lost an ear.'

'An ear?' Stephen picked up the paper, crossed to the window and held it at an angle so light fell on it. It was dusk, and the only illumination in the room came from the TV screen. He hoped he looked cooler than he felt.

There it was in black and white. YOUTH MUTI-LATED IN KNIFE ATTACK. Maxwell hadn't exaggerated, then. He skimmed the story. *Jarnal Singh, sixteen, set upon by a knife-wielding man as he walked with two friends to the Valley to watch United's game against Burnley. Cuts to hands and face. Left ear severed, though surgeons at Shadderton Royal Infirmary managed to stitch this back in place. Attacker, who got away, described as white, five foot eleven, wearing black leather jacket and blue jeans. Police are anxious to interview anyone who might have witnessed . . . bla bla bla . . .*

Stephen's hands were shaking. He inhaled slowly, thankful the others were glued to the box. Maxwell's words played back in his skull. *I'd hate to have to slice off one of your lugs.* But you'd do it, wouldn't you, Brian? he thought. You'd actually do it.

There was another bit to the story. In fact, it was a different story only they'd run the two together. *In a separate incident, two thirteen-year-old boys were badly beaten in an empty house on Raglan Street. Both were taken to Shadderton Royal Infirmary where their condition was said to be comfortable.* Oh sure. Nothing like a bad beating to make you feel comfortable. Stephen left the paper on the window sill and crossed to the door. On screen, United were repeating their four nil demolition of Burnley. He didn't stay to watch.

FORTY-THREE

Waseem Kader took a seat in the front row and looked at the two photos pinned to the wall. One was a fuzzy black and white blow-up of a youth's head swathed in bandages. All you could see of him was his eyes and the mute question in them – why? Why me? The other, also fuzzy, was of Rehana Majid, crescent scar like a lopsided smile on her chin.

Basir Khan, alone this time behind the table, called the meeting to order. He'd counted fifty-six people. A good turnout. He caught Waseem's eye and nodded.

The blow-ups had been his idea, and a good one. The audience was fired up, ready for whatever might be asked of it.

'The boy with the bandaged head', he began softly, 'is Jarnal Singh, a Sikh. Some of you may know him, most of you will have seen the piece about him in the *Post*. For the benefit of those who don't and haven't, let me tell you that Jarnal was attacked last Saturday by a white man with a knife as he was making his way to The Valley to watch a football match. He wasn't doing anything wrong, just walking along minding his business.' Basir Khan paused to steeple his fingers and rest his chin on them. 'Now there may be those among you who will say, Jarnal Singh is no concern of ours. He is a Sikh. Let his own people worry about him. To those people I say, Jarnal was not attacked because he was a Sikh. The creatures who carry out assaults of this sort make no distinction between Sikh and Muslim, or Hindu for that matter. They look at a person from the subcontinent and see a Paki.' He lowered his hands to the table top and made fists of them. 'Paki. That's what the knifeman said as he sliced off this boy's ear. "How d'you like it, Paki?" So you see, it *is* our affair, whether we like it or not. The second picture shows Rehana Majid who you all know, scarred for life for the same crime – being a Paki.'

There was a pitcher and glass at the speaker's elbow. Basir poured himself a drink and sipped, giving his listeners opportunity to talk among themselves. They would massage one another's anger and they were going to need their anger. *He* needed it. He let three minutes slip by, then cleared his throat.

'The two assaults I have spoken of have one thing in common, namely that nobody has been charged. As is so often the case where racial attacks are concerned, the police appear strangely reluctant, strangely slow to react. It is as though they don't really *want* to catch those responsible, which perhaps they don't. So.' He smiled thinly. 'It seems it is up to ourselves to see justice done, and in fact this process has already commenced. Those of you who read the *Post* may have seen a piece about two boys being beaten in a derelict house. Those are the boys who attacked, robbed and disfigured Rehana Majid, and those who beat them are in this room tonight.'

Cheers and applause followed this revelation. Basir Khan had anticipated this and waited, smiling and nodding till it subsided. 'This was a beginning only. The real struggle commences the day after tomorrow, when the Butt family faces forcible removal from its home in Cardigan Street, which is due for demolition. The family has been allocated a flat on the Brockbank Estate but wishes to remain where it is. Khalifa believes this wish to be fair and reasonable and intends to support it by occupying the house and refusing to leave. It is easy to clap and cheer, less easy to place your body between a bulldozer and a brick wall. A register will now be circulated. If you have been playing, go home. Playtime is over. If you are serious, sign up.'

When the register was returned to the table it bore fifty-six signatures. Nobody had been playing.

FORTY-FOUR

Tuesday morning. Brother and sister left the house together, then split up. Since his refusal to speak up for Ashraf, Colleen had stopped walking with Stephen. There was more than one route to school. Colleen would take the direct route, often meeting up with Abida along the way, while Stephen took the footpath across the rec. It was a pleasant walk which gave him time to think.

This morning there was a yellow mini at the kerb where the footpath began. As Stephen drew near the driver stuck out her head. 'Excuse me?'

'Yes?' He supposed she wanted directions.

'You're Stephen Crowley, aren't you?'

'Ye-es.' How the heck does she know? Who is she?

'Name's Jennifer Most. I'm with the *Post*.' She grinned. 'I always feel like I'm starting a rap when I say that. Have you got a minute?'

'Well – I'm on my way to school, but if it *is* just a minute . . .'

'It is. Hang on while I get out of this sardine tin.'

He watched her get out. Not bad looking. Green eyes with a smile in them. Chestnut hair cut short. Nice legs. Impossible to get out of a mini and not show plenty of leg. Age? twenty-one, twenty-two. He finger-combed his hair, wishing he wasn't in uniform.

'Right.' She straightened her skirt, flicked the ends of the silk scarf, looked around. 'Shame there's nowhere to sit. We could . . .' She indicated the car. He shook his head.

'No time. What d'you want? How d'you know my name?'

She looked at him. 'I talked to a couple named Khan, Saturday, for a feature I'm doing. Your name cropped up.'

'Cropped up?' He frowned. 'How exactly?'

'They have a son. Ashraf. I met him briefly in his parents' shop. He's in trouble with the law and his father seems to think you could help him, but won't. I promised Mr Khan I'd –'

Stephen shook his head. 'You're wasting your time. I don't know anything about it. I wasn't even there. I'd better be off or I'll be late.'

'You *were* there, Stephen.'

'No I wasn't, and how the heck would you know anyway?'

'I know because I was there too and I saw you.'

'Did you heck! Why would you be there? I'd have . . .'

'Seen me?' She smiled. 'How, if you weren't there yourself?'

'OK.' Stephen raised his hands, palms forward. 'I was there. I admit it, but I couldn't help Ashraf Khan even if I wanted to, which I don't. It'd be more than my life's worth.'

The reporter gazed at him. 'You're afraid, aren't you, Stephen?'

He flushed, shook his head. 'No, I'm not afraid of anything. I just can't be seen siding with . . . with . . .'

'A Paki? Is that what you're trying to say? You daren't side with Ashraf Khan for fear of what your friends might say. Your Blackout friends, that is.'

'It's not what they'll *say*, you stupid cow. It's what they'll *do*. You don't know. They're . . .'

'Crazy?'

'No. No, they're . . . determined. Dedicated. They stick together. They expect –'

'They're crazy, Stephen. Crazy, violent and deeply ignorant, while you – you're an A level candidate for goodness' sake! You don't belong with those people. *Think*. Use your –'

'It's me that's crazy,' spat Stephen, 'standing here listening to you when you don't understand anything. I'm off.' He swung his sport bag over his shoulder, turned and hurried away down the footpath. Jennifer Most called after him. 'If you need me, Stephen, if ever you want to talk, you know where to find me.' He didn't look back.

FORTY-FIVE

Wednesday. A cold September dawn. Basir Khan and Idris Butt stood on Butt's doorstep. 'Your wife and daughters – they're somewhere safe?'

'I sent them to my wife's brother. Only my son is here.'

Khan nodded. 'Good.' He looked at his watch. Six thirty. 'The others will start arriving soon. Meanwhile let me see the layout of the house. We must secure all doors, all windows. Is there a coal chute?'

The two men went inside. Mist drifted in rags over damp cobbles, blurring the outlines of abandoned houses. A thin cat paused to investigate an empty tin and stalked on, its gait suggestive more of resignation than of disappointment.

At six thirty-two, two men appeared, making for the only house in Cardigan Street with a lighted window. They went inside. Moments later two more approached from the opposite direction. Suddenly the street seemed filled with young men in jeans and mufflers, converging on the light. The cat, preferring its own company, trotted up an entry and slipped into a property whose last day had dawned.

At seven, the silence of the doomed street was broken by the growl and roar of powerful motors. On giant tyres and caterpillar tracks came bulldozers, cranes with chains and iron balls, and truckloads of men in donkey jackets, boots and knitted caps. Gouts of blue exhaust mingled with the mist. Voices shouted to and fro. There was no messing. Starting at number one, the wrecking crew proceeded to smash walls which had stood for a century. Roofs that had kept the rain off four generations of Shaddertonians buckled, broke and fell, sending slate avalanches crashing into cellars where people had sheltered from the bombs of two world wars. Everybody's taste in wallpaper endured brief exposure then toppled, slabs of green, pink and yellow falling into a chaos of dust and rubble. Hurry, hurry, hurry was the order of the day. 1999 was coming, with the Millennium right behind.

Inside number forty-three, tense but unafraid, waited the warriors of Khalifa. Though all the might was with the enemy, right was on their side and so, ins'Allah, they would win.

At ten o'clock, with the iron balls a mere five doors away, silence fell. A group of men approached the door of forty-three. Some wore suits, others were in police uniform. A sergeant knocked loudly. Getting no response he tried the door. It was locked. There was a letter slot. The sergeant bent down, opened the slot and called through it. 'Mr Butt, twenty-eight days ago you were served notice to vacate these premises. Alternative accommodation was offered. All proper procedures have been followed. This house is due for demolition today. You have five minutes in which to come out. If you persist in remaining inside I shall have no alternative but to order my men to remove you by force, in which case you may be charged with obstruction. Now, sir – will you come out?' As the officer straightened up, a single, muffled word came from beyond the door.

'Never.'

FORTY-SIX

'Ashraf Khan.' After a brief, *sotto voce* consultation with the colleagues either side of him, the presiding magistrate was peering at Ashraf over his half-glasses. 'You have been found guilty of possession of an offensive weapon – a most serious offence, and one which has in recent years become all too common.' He paused. Faintly from outside, voices could be heard chanting, though the words themselves were unintelligible. The magistrate cleared his throat and continued. 'Society has the right to expect protection from the mindless violence of a minority of vicious individuals, and for this reason I would not hesitate normally to impose a custodial sentence. However, having taken into account your previous impeccable record, and the esteem in which you are evidently held by the head-master of your school, I am going to sentence you to six months imprisonment, suspended for two years.' An outburst of cheering from the public benches was extinguished at once by the magistrate's gavel. 'Any more of that', he rasped, 'and I'll clear the court.' He turned to Ashraf. 'Do you understand what a suspended sentence means, young man?'

Ashraf shook his head. 'No, sir, not really.'

'Then I'll tell you. It does *not* mean you've *got off*, as the expression has it. It means in your case that should you be found guilty of any offence during the next two years, you will serve the six months imposed today *in addition* to any penalty imposed in respect of the new offence. Do you understand *that*?'

'Yessir.'

'Then you're free to go.'

FORTY-SEVEN

Friday, first period. Religious Knowledge with Mr Nation, nickname Dam. Year Ten was studying Judaism. Colleen leaned towards Abida. 'I'm glad Ash didn't get prison, Abi. Really glad. Your mum and dad must be relieved.'

Abida nodded, one eye on the teacher. 'Yes they are, but Dad's dead worried in case Waseem gets Ash mixed up with Khalifa again. He's in that house, you know. Cardigan Street.'

'The *siege*?'

'Yes.'

'Ooh heck! I was reading about that in the paper. Somebody's going to get killed if that goes on.'

'I know. And if Ash joins in and gets arrested, it's jail and that's it. Dad'll never let him back if that happens.'

'Hmm. Just have to hope –'

'Colleen Crowley.' Dam glared. 'Perhaps *you* can tell us which Jewish festival took place last Tuesday?'

'Uh . . . was it Pesach, sir?'

'Pesach was in April, Colleen. This is September. You can always tell when it's September because you've

103

just had the summer holidays. Remember the holidays, do you?'

'Yessir.'

'Ah – then it's not *total* amnesia. Have you any recollection of last Friday?'

'F–Friday, sir?'

'Ah-ha. Often follows Thursday, for some reason. Do you remember sitting in this classroom last Friday, listening to me banging on about something called the Day of Atonement?'

'Er – I think so, sir, yes.'

The teacher beamed. 'Splendid. So gratifying to know one's efforts are not *totally* wasted. I'm pushing my luck here I know, but do you by any chance remember the *name* of that festival?'

'No, sir.'

Dam sighed. 'I knew I was pushing it. What about you, Abida?'

'Yom Kippur, sir.'

'Yom Kippur is the correct answer. Well done, Abida.' He gazed at the two girls. 'If the pair of you can bear to suspend the conversation you were having till break, then who knows – you *might* remember some fragment of today's session next week, which would be really nice.' He turned and scrawled YOM KIPPUR on the board. The lesson continued.

FORTY-EIGHT

'Steve?'

'Yes?' Stephen's response was so eager he almost said
'sir'. Well, it's not every Friday night you're appointed
second in command, Number One Commando.
Martin Lawson indicated the door. 'Just make sure
those two're on their toes, will you? Don't want any
earwiggers, tonight of all nights.'

'Right.' Stephen opened the door, peered into the
dim corridor. The two sentries were sitting on the top
step, playing cards. They looked round as the door
opened. One, fag in mouth, raised his eyebrows. 'Help
you, kid, can we?'

'Yes. Martin wants you on your toes.'

'We're on 'em, baby face.'

'You're not, you're on your bums. And don't call
me baby face.' His cheek amazed him. It seemed to
surprise the sentries too. The smoker got slowly to
his feet, eyeballing the boy through a blue fug. His
companion gathered up the cards, taking his time.
Stephen waited. The youth knocked the pack into a
block, dropped them in their box and stood up, slipping
the box in his jeans pocket. He gazed at Stephen. 'You

better pray', he drawled, 'that you never run into me and Dean when you're by yourself, 'cause if you do it'll be *your* toes we're on, not ours. Tell Martin everything's fine.'

He closed the door, nodded at Martin and resumed his seat. Now that everybody knew which commando they were in, the subject of the siege was raised. The Siege of Cardigan Street, the *Post* was calling it. It was in its third day, and everybody present was of the opinion that the authorities were being too soft with the occupants of number forty-three. '*I'd* get 'em out,' growled Brian Maxwell. 'Two minutes flat.'

'Yeah,' grinned the man sitting next to him. 'But the cops want 'em out *alive*.' Everybody laughed except Wendy Shoesmith, who said, 'Yeah, well that's it, isn't it? They're *always* soft on blacks. Daren't be anything else or they're racist, aren't they? Look how that Paki got off – six months, suspended. If that'd been one of us, we'd be inside now. I say it's time we *did* something about that siege.'

'Yeah, but . . .' Stephen flushed as eyes turned towards him. He hadn't meant to speak. Rank's gone to my head, he thought, fleetingly. Like a brand new prefect at school.

Wendy glared at him. 'Yeah but *what*?'

'Well – what we're here for – I mean what I *thought* that we were doing was trying to stop this Millennium Development thing.'

'Yeah. So?'

'So this siege is holding it up, right? We're on the same side in a way, us and this Khalifa mob.'

'No!' Out front, Martin Lawson shook his head. 'No, son. No, no, no. Never on the same side. Never. See – it's not only *what* gets done, it's *who* gets it done, and by whom. I mean, us beating the council . . . *us*, Blackout, that's one thing. That's white against white, see? That's democracy. It's the way things work. The way they've always worked. But *blacks* defying the authorities . . . the white authorities – the authorities that represent you and me and everybody here – that's a different matter altogether. When it comes to something like that, it's us and the authorities against them. *Has* to be, otherwise, anarchy. No. On this particular occasion, son, it's our role to *assist* the council, even if the council isn't aware that it needs our assistance.' He smiled. 'And that, my son, is where Number One Commando comes in. Listen.'

FORTY-NINE

Sonia Crowley spoke from behind the family's copy of the *Post*. 'Good piece here about the Khans. How the parents got here. What their life was like before.

Funny to think of people leaving a way of life that disappeared here three, four hundred years ago and finding themselves a couple of days later in sixties Shadderton. Like travelling forward in time.'

'Or back,' said Colleen. 'I bet they didn't get people shut up in a house with folks outside threatening to smash it in with iron balls.'

'There are far worse things than that in Pakistan,' put in Michael, setting a tray on the coffee table. It was ten fifteen, time for hot chocolate. 'Drought, famine, epidemic, unstable government. The sort of things we haven't had here for centuries.'

Stephen, who had just got home, nodded. 'They're laughing, what with water that comes out of taps and the NHS. And if they don't like it they should go back where they came from, not barricade themselves in houses, breaking the law.'

'You're racist,' accused Colleen. 'You've been reading that Lawson creep who keeps writing to the paper.'

'I have not!' retorted Stephen. 'I think about things, not like some people I could mention.' He looked at his mother. 'Who's written it? Someone called Jennifer Most, I'll bet.'

His mother nodded. 'That's right, dear. How did you know?'

He shrugged. 'She stopped me in the street the other day because I know Ashraf. Thought we were mates. She doesn't . . . mention me, does she?'

'No. It's just a feature about an ordinary Shadderton family. First in a series, it says. Here.' She held out the paper. 'Read it with your chocolate.'

Stephen shook his head. 'Can't, Mum. Got to go out again.'

'Out?' His father frowned. 'It's twenty-past ten, Stephen. You've only just walked in. What's so important you have to go dashing off at this time of night?'

He was ready for this one. Had rehearsed it walking home, keeping an eye open for Phil and Dean. 'I promised somebody, Dad.' He did his bashful bit. 'Actually it's . . . a girl.'

'Ah.' Michael nodded. 'I see. Well, don't . . . don't stay out too late, will you? This girl's parents – they'll worry, you know. Where do they live, anyway?'

'Oh . . . not far. Leave the chocolate. I'll microwave it when I get back. See you.'

'Bye, son. Don't do anything I wouldn't do.'

FIFTY

A few weeks ago Stephen had watched a fifties western on TV. One of the minor characters was an ancient guy whose caved-in mouth boasted one last tooth. Cardigan Street looked like that mouth, number forty-three jutting alone from drifts and heaps of rubble. The street lamps had gone. The only light came from the windows of forty-three, and from the moon. Stephen stood in the shadow of a truck, waiting for the others.

There were three in Number One Commando besides himself. Brian Maxwell was leader. The others were two guys named Kev and Pete, whom he didn't really know. They were both older than Stephen but had seemed not to mind when Martin made the boy second in command. Like most people they were followers, not leaders.

Brian arrived on foot, carrying nothing. Stephen whispered, 'Where are . . . I thought we . . .'

'Sssh!' Maxwell peered along the street. 'We are. Kev and Pete are fetching 'em.' He grinned, his teeth gleaming in the dark. 'Serious offence, possessing those things. Us leaders can't afford to be nabbed with 'em.'

After a few minutes they heard a vehicle approaching. It stopped short of Cardigan Street and presently the two men appeared, overloaded pockets pulling their jackets out of shape. They stopped on the littered cobbles. 'Brian?'

'Ssssh! Over here.' The pair joined Stephen and Brian by the truck. Brian looked at them. 'Any trouble?'

'Naw. Bit of ring road traffic. No fuzz. Where d'you want −?'

'Put 'em on the deck. How many?'

'Four, like you said.'

'Where'd you get the bottles?'

'Different places. Skips. Doorsteps.'

'*Doorsteps?*'

Pete grinned. 'Yeah. One's a milk bottle.'

'OK. And the petrol – you filled a can?'

'Sure, don't worry. We used Kev's van for the filling station and my banger for getting here, just like you told us.'

'Good.' Maxwell squatted, picking up each bottle in turn, fingering the strips of rag stuffed in their necks. Stephen watched, fighting to stop the trembling in his limbs. Molotov cocktail. Jokey name, deadly missile. He remembered the news once, some guy got eight years for throwing one. Eight years. Suppose . . . suppose there was a police guard watching the house? There might be. It was a siege after all. If there *was* a guard, there might not be time to get away. Oh, Martin had sussed everything out, or said he had. Stephen knew exactly what he had to do after he threw his bomb. There was an alleyway twenty metres beyond the house, linking Cardigan Street to Balaclava Place. He was to take this alleyway, then stroll off down Balaclava Place as if nothing had happened and make his way home. Easy for Martin to say. Martin, who was sitting at home right now waiting for Brian to call when the job was done. Brian had a different escape route. So had Kev and Pete, but what if things had changed since Martin reconnoitred the area? For instance, what if this famous alleyway was now blocked with rubble, or there was a dirty great hole in the middle of it, waiting to plunge him into a sewer or cellar? Take your pick, you lucky guy – eight years or a broken neck.

'Right.' Brian straightened up. 'Bottle in right hand, lighter in left. Walk, don't run. Kev – yours is the lighted window this side. Me and Pete hit the front – Pete the upstairs window, me the door panel. Steve, you do the window on the far side. Listen for my whistle, light your fuse and throw. Stay cool and you can't miss, but don't wait around to watch what happens and *don't* throw your lighter down. Put it in your pocket. And if one of us is caught, he was working alone and has never heard of Blackout. Got all that?' They nodded. Brian picked up a bottle. The others did likewise. Stephen fished the green disposable lighter from his pocket. What if it wouldn't light? What if the bomb went off in his hand? What if a sentry saw them coming? Brian had left the shadow of the truck and was striding towards the house. No more time for what-ifs. Eight years though, for if-onlys. Stephen gulped and moved forward, Kev and Pete at his heels.

FIFTY-ONE

'Jennifer Most?' A man's voice, unfamiliar.

'Yes. Who's this?'

'A concerned citizen. In view of your sympathetic piece on the Khans, I thought you'd be interested to know that number forty-three Cardigan Street will be fire-bombed in the next few minutes.'

'Who *are* you? How do you know this? What can *I* do about it?'

'Call the police. If they're quick they might even nab a bomber or two.' The man chuckled. 'Or you could get over there yourself. You know, "Our reporter on the spot." Look good in tomorrow's paper, that would. G'night.'

The lighter worked first go. As Stephen touched the flame to the rag, holding the bottle at arm's length, there was a crash of breaking glass followed immediately by a flash. Somebody cried out. He heard voices inside the house, shouting. More glass shattered. An orange glow pulsated to his left, swelling. His fuse was burning now, yellow flame climbing hungrily towards the bottle neck. He drew back his arm and threw without aiming.

The bottle arced through the air trailing sparks, missed the window by at least a metre and burst against the wall. Flame blossomed on stone. Thin streams of fire ran like lava down the house side. Stephen turned and ran, not caring that he'd missed, caring only about the alleyway and his escape.

It was there, and it wasn't blocked. He pelted between twin ridges of heaped rubble, swung left on to Balaclava Place and forced himself to slow to a walk, though his heart continued to race. The houses here were still standing, but all were empty. Through glassless windows he glimpsed the fire he'd helped start. He was passing it now. There was shouting, so at least some of the occupiers must have got out. He hoped they all had. He hoped Brian, Pete and Kev were safely away. He prayed nobody was tailing him. He cursed himself for a fool.

FIFTY-TWO

Watching his mug revolve in the microwave, he'd heard sirens. Fire sirens, police sirens. Ambulance sirens? God no, not that. A house – a house that was coming down anyway – that's one thing. Disfiguring somebody, maiming – that's different. And what about *killing*?

He'd gulped his chocolate, then thrown up in the

sink. Good job everybody else was in bed. He'd hurried off to bed himself but not to sleep. A knock on the door was what he'd mostly thought about. A loud, authoritative knock with the majesty of the law behind it. It hadn't come but it had kept him awake anyway, and of course it wasn't too late. It might come now, as he was pulling on his sock. Now, as he zombied down the stairs to join the others at a breakfast that might easily end up like last night's chocolate. Now, as he walked in the kitchen.

They were smiling, all three of them. He nodded, sat down and reached for the cornflakes. It wasn't till his father said, 'Well – and how did the two of you get on?' that he remembered they thought he'd had a date last night. A date with one girl, not three psychopaths. *That's* what the daft grins were in aid of. He shrugged, forced a wan smile. 'OK, I guess.'

'Well – who *is* she?' This from his mother. 'Do we know her? Is she somebody at school?'

'N-no.' He shook his head. 'She works.'

'Oh – where, dear? What does she do?'

'Sandoz. She's at Sandoz, but I'm not sure what she does. Lab Tech, maybe.'

'Oooh – a scientist. Looks *and* brains, eh?'

'Huh!' grunted Colleen. 'She can't have much of either if she'll meet *him* at half ten at night.'

'That's a bit unkind, dear,' reproved her mother. 'You know nothing about this girl.'

'No.' Colleen shook her head. 'Funny, that.'

During this exchange the paper had thudded on to the mat and Michael had risen to fetch it. As Stephen poured milk on his cornflakes he resumed his seat, unfolded the *Post* and exclaimed, 'Good grief!'

'What is it, dear?' Stephen, who knew exactly what it was, slopped milk on the bar top. Michael answered from behind the paper. 'The siege, love. Cardigan Street. It's over. Somebody firebombed the house last night. Gutted, apparently.'

'Oh, Michael! Was anybody hurt?'

'Dunno. I'm reading.'

Stephen got up, brought a cloth and dabbed at the spilled milk. His mother tut-tutted at the mess he'd made and he wondered fleetingly what she'd say if she saw what he could do with petrol. He wished his father would hurry up and answer her question, which was far more important to him than to her. He held the cloth under the tap and wrung it out, trying to appear mildly interested.

'No,' grunted Michael, after what felt like a fortnight. 'There were seventeen men in the house and they all escaped unhurt. Fireman reckons it's miraculous, and I bet the council's chuffed on the quiet as well, though of course they condemn the violence.' He chuckled. 'It's saved 'em a whole lot of bother though, that violence. A cynic might wonder if they had something to do with it.'

'A cynic', murmured Colleen as she passed the sugar to her white-faced brother, 'might wonder why two people who like each other would make a date for half-past ten when they might just as easily be together by half-past eight.'

FIFTY-THREE

Monday, eight forty-five. Cheers and applause rang out from over by the gateway. The two girls, deep in conversation near old Pelham's Volvo, glanced towards the sound. Ashraf, returning to school for the first time since his court appearance, came grinning into the yard to the acclaim of a knot of Pakistani pupils. Abida groaned. 'They're making a hero of him. Father was afraid something like this might happen. He wanted to keep Ash at home another week but Mother said he must come to school, it's the law.'

Colleen nodded. 'Stephen would have his fans too if they knew what he did Friday night.'

Abida looked at her. 'Friday night? You don't mean . . . ?'

'I think so. He went out. Late. Some tale about a girl. Everybody was in bed when he got back. I can't prove it of course, but I think he was there. You

should've seen him at breakfast Saturday, looking terrified. I'm amazed Mum and Dad didn't notice.'

Ashraf's friends had hoisted him on their shoulders
and were trotting him round the yard, whooping and
laughing. As they passed the staff entrance the door
flew open and Pelham came out. 'Stop!' he roared.
The knot of boys slowed, wheeled in the Head's direction, and stood looking at him. Pelham nodded towards
Ashraf. 'Put that boy down.' They hesitated and he
snapped, 'Now!'

Ashraf was lowered to the ground. The Head gazed
at him. 'I shall want to see you in my office straight
after registration. The rest of you had better reflect on
what I said a week last Wednesday about our school.
What *did* I say, Rasool Akhtar?'

The boy frowned and stared at the asphalt, shuffling
his feet. Pelham looked at him. 'I'm waiting, lad.'

'I . . . dunno, sir.'

'Then I'll remind you. I said our school is a community. *One* community, in which we are all sisters
and brothers. *What* are we, Rasool?'

'Sir, sisters and brothers.'

'That's right, and don't you forget it. Any of you. I
won't have students chaired round this yard for hooli-
ganism or lawless behaviour of any sort. We reserve
that privilege for those who bring honour, not shame
to the name of Shadderton Comprehensive. Get along
now. And don't forget our appointment, Ashraf Khan.'

FIFTY-FOUR

'Now, Ashraf.' Pelham gazed up at the boy from his swivel chair. 'What is it, eh? What's going on? You're one of the most conscientious students this school has ever had. You're in Year Twelve, heading for university. You've got a bright future ahead of you and suddenly *bang*! Out of the blue I get a call from your father who tells me you're under arrest. What on earth's got into you, lad?'

'Sir, I . . . I don't want to sound cheeky or anything, but I couldn't explain to you because it's an Islamic thing. You wouldn't understand.'

The Head looked at him. 'Try me, Ashraf.'

'Well, sir . . . it all boils down to this Millennium Development. Some people – the council, I suppose – see the development as a way of, like, welding the people of Shadderton into a single community. You know – sisters and brothers, like you want to do here in school, but not everybody thinks that'd be a good thing. Like, one of the things they're planning is one big campus where kids'll go to school from five to sixteen or eighteen. White kids, Asians, everybody, but our imam believes Muslim kids – especially girls

– should have their own schools so they won't be influenced by . . . well –' Ashraf shrugged. '– white girls, sir – *some* white girls are brought up . . . differently from Muslim girls. Boyfriends and that. No . . .'

'No moral supervision?' supplied the Head.

Ashraf nodded. 'Something like that, sir, yes. And there's other stuff. All sorts of things the imam mentions in his . . . his sermons.'

Pelham shifted in his chair. 'This imam. I take it you're referring to Imam Hassan Salaam, the man whose name's been in the papers a lot?'

Ashraf nodded. 'Yessir.'

'The man who supports the fatwa on Salman Rushdie, among other things?'

'Yessir.'

'Well, you know . . .' Pelham frowned, toying with a ballpoint on his desk. 'There are many Muslims, Ashraf – and I'm talking about *devout* Muslims – who strongly disagree with Imam Hassan Salaam. I was at a dinner recently talking to a man – a practising Muslim and a respected figure here in Shadderton – who said to me, "Mine is a beautiful religion, but the trouble is that some of its practitioners make up rules to suit themselves."' He looked up at the boy. 'We were talking about your imam at the time.'

Ashraf didn't say anything but stood, staring at the Head's cluttered desktop. Yes, Islam has its factions, he thought. Its denominations. Not every Muslim believes exactly the same thing, but that's true of all religions. It's so complicated, most *Muslims* don't understand it all, so how can you hope to explain to an outsider? In the end all you can say is, *I've got my beliefs, you've got yours, and they don't mix.* And that's why the Bennett Qureshi Millennium development won't work. They don't mix.

'Listen, Ashraf.' Pelham gazed at him. '*I* don't believe you went armed to that . . . confrontation, but you went, and if you keep that sort of company you needn't be surprised when you're judged by their standards. Brawling, even for religious reasons, doesn't make a man a hero, it makes him a thug, and we don't honour thugs at Shadderton Comprehensive. So.' Pelham clasped his hands on the desktop. 'I want you to forget about politics, Ashraf, including religious politics, and get down to some hard work. You've damaged your reputation, lad, but it's not beyond repair. Not if you knuckle down now and get those A levels under your belt. Make your parents proud of you, not ashamed. Make *us* proud, and above all take a pride in *yourself.* You've got it in you, so use it. Off you go.'

FIFTY-FIVE

'I knew it. I *knew* that nephew of mine would stir up a hornets' nest. Listen to this.' Hassan folded the paper at the letters page, smoothed it out and read:

'"Sir

I was angered and dismayed by Councillor Kenneth Coxmoor's recent letter, in which he condemned the firebombing of number forty-three Cardigan Street as an act of mindless criminality. He referred to those responsible as brain-dead monsters, and suggested that if they are caught they should be jailed for life. Attentive readers will have noticed that Mr Coxmoor had nothing whatever to say about the hooligan rabble which occupied the house in the first place. While it goes without saying that every responsible Shaddertonian condemns the bombing, natural justice demands that we do not lose sight of the fact that it was their unlawful action which led to it. These people escaped with their lives and we are all thankful for that, but they broke the law just as surely as did the bombers, and they must not go unpunished. What's sauce for the goose . . ."'

Ashraf stared into his lap and said nothing. Abida, clearing the table, said, 'Who wrote that letter, Daddy?'

'It is signed Russell Pollinger. He's a Councillor too, you know. In the debate about the Millennium Development they were on the same side, now they are at each other's throat. That's what happens when people resort to violence.' He began to summarize the letter in Urdu for his wife's benefit. Abida carried bowls and mats through to the kitchen. Ashraf sighed. Lectures all flipping day at school, lectures all flipping night at home. He got up and headed for the stairs.

FIFTY-SIX

'Our first bit of business tonight is to congratulate Number One Commando on the terrific job it did last Friday.'

'Hear! Hear!' The upper room of the Waggon and Horses exploded into a roar that could be heard in the bar downstairs. Martin Lawson smiled. Stephen stared modestly at the floor, aglow with pleasure. A week had passed, the police had expended their best efforts and the knock he'd dreaded hadn't come. It wouldn't now. He was free to enjoy his hero status.

'Thanks to Brian, Steve, Kev and Peter,' continued

Lawson, 'Cardigan Street no longer exists. It's a wilderness of rubble, and some day soon every street in every Paki ghetto in England will be the same.' A second roar. 'We'll split 'em up, and when they're split up, we'll pick 'em off one by one. By the time we've finished with 'em, they'll be queuing up at Heathrow for planes back to Pakistan.'

This time the racket went on for over a minute as pumped-up members stamped, cheered and slapped one another on the shoulder. Lawson sat, fists on table-top, till it faded, then murmured, 'Tonight, Number Two Commando gets the chance to show what it can do. In this parcel . . .' He bent, lifted an irregularly-shaped and apparently heavy brown paper parcel and placed it on the table. 'In this parcel is not a bomb as some of you are probably thinking, but something just as explosive if it's placed in the right spot, and that's Two Commando's task for tonight.' He looked up. 'Wendy, Phil, Roger and Dean – you'll stay behind after for briefing, please. As I said it's not a bomb, but it's a ticklish job just the same. OK.' He smiled. 'Next item, treasurer's report, and I can tell you there's good news on that front too.'

FIFTY-SEVEN

The mosque whose gilded dome now dominated Carlyle Road had risen slowly over twelve years. Each brick, every trowelful of cement had been paid for in advance by voluntary subscription. Its foundations had been laid when some of Shadderton's mills were still open, and at first the work had proceeded quite rapidly. Then, as factory after factory paid off its employees and closed its gates for the last time, the project slowed to a trickle. Sometimes it dried up altogether, and for weeks on end no work was done on the site. By the time the soaring, slender minaret was finished and the muezzin proclaimed the hour of prayer for the first time from its balcony, many of the mosque's original subscribers were dead. Now, however, it stood gleaming in white, green and gold among rundown shops and rows of terraced houses whose occupants had paid for it. Even this misty October midnight could not shroud its magnificence.

Wendy Shoesmith crouched with her companions in the shadow of a rusting skip outside the gutted shell of a former shop, fifty metres from the mosque. Except for the occasional passing taxi, the four had the road to themselves. Wendy looked at her second in command.

'The door's obviously a non-starter, Phil. Solid as a rock, so it'll have to be a window. We can't force one or use the glass cutter because they're set too high, so all we can do is heave a brick through one and chuck this after it.' She indicated the parcel. 'That means noise, which means we'll need to get the hell out of here straight after, and I mean *seconds* after.' She glanced at each of the others. 'You don't need me to tell you what'll happen to anyone they catch once we've done it. So. Phil – you'll go back to the car, start her up and be ready for a quick getaway. You two.' She looked at Roger and Dean. 'Choose a brick apiece. There's a skipful behind you. When I give the word, you run to within chucking distance and throw. The reason for two bricks is, one might miss, but *don't* let it be you or I'll see Martin gets to know about it. Roger – you'll take the first window this side. Dean – yours is the one next to it. As soon as your brick's away, run for the car. Don't wait for each other, and don't wait for me. I'll be right behind you. I'm unwrapping the parcel now. I'll pick a window and chuck Percy here through the hole. If I miss I'll try again, and I'll keep on trying till the thing goes in, but if I'm not back at the car one minute after you, go without me and I mean that. If I'm nicked I'll say I was working alone – Blackout knows nothing about it.'

She checked that Phil had gone, and that the others

had selected their missiles. 'OK.' A final peep round the end of the skip. All clear. 'Go!' The two men burst from the shadow, pelted along the pavement and hurled their bricks. Two green-framed windows exploded, the sound magnified by the stillness of the night. Wendy Shoesmith sprinted towards the building, selected the window with the larger hole and tossed her bloody burden at it. The pig's head sailed through the jagged gap as the woman turned and fled.

FIFTY-EIGHT

Friday's *Post* had carried the second 'Most in the Post' piece, based on an interview with the Bishop of Shadderton. In it the prelate had spoken of his optimism about race relations in the town, which he believed were less strained than the media's recent coverage might suggest, and which would be even better once the Millennium Development was completed.

O. B. Stocks had been delighted by the piece, and had said so to Jennifer Most. 'We're showing people, the Bishop included, that not *all* of the media is irresponsible,' he'd said. 'If His Grace's optimism turns out to be justified, we at the *Post* will have done our little bit.'

Saturday's edition stood in stark contrast. MILLION POUND MOSQUE DEFILED, read the banner headline. 'Unclean forever' claim. The story beneath the headline was both brief and grim. Awoken by the sound of breaking glass, the mosque's caretaker, whose house stood a few metres from the building, had rushed to his window in time to see somebody running off along Carlyle Road. Pulling on some clothes he'd hurried across to the mosque, half expecting to find the place on fire. Instead, on opening the door and turning on some lights he'd seen an object in the middle of the floor. Approaching it he'd been sickened to recognize the head of a pig. The head had obviously been thrown through one of two broken windows, and because there were two he'd spent some minutes searching for a second head before running back to his house to call the police. There was only the one head, but it had rolled a considerable distance across the floor, leaving traces of itself on the tiles. The police had found two bricks and a lot of broken glass, but no clue as to who might be responsible. Enquiries, said a spokesperson, were being vigorously pursued.

Khalifa's spokesman, who asked that his name be withheld, was less formal. 'We've a fair idea who's behind this filthy act,' he said, 'and the minute we prove it, he's dead.'

Martin Lawson slept badly that Saturday night.

FIFTY-NINE

Stephen didn't have a good night either, and it wasn't only because United had lost at home. Khalifa's vow to kill the defilers of the mosque had shaken him more than he was prepared to admit, even to himself. *We've a fair idea who's behind this filthy act.* What if they thought it was *him*? Well – he'd bombed the house in Cardigan Street because Martin Lawson told him to, hadn't he? And if Martin had given that job to Number Two Commando and the mosque to his lot, he *would* be behind it, wouldn't he? In which case he'd be under sentence of death right now. And besides, Khalifa might not just be talking about the people who actually did the job. They might mean Blackout as a whole. Suppose they decide to wipe the lot of us out?

Not a good night.

Ashraf slept surprisingly well, considering his parents and sister had moved to Brockbank that day and he'd refused to go with them. 'I'm not coming,' he'd announced at breakfast. It was the family's last meal at the shop – a sad occasion which his decision did nothing to lighten. There'd been a flaming row of course – his father had ended by *ordering* his son to obey him, but it's not like that any more. Not in 1998, and not in England. 'I'm over sixteen,' the boy had replied. 'I can live anywhere I like.' Which is true.

He'd moved in with his cousin, of course. Waseem had a flat in a big house on the edge of Shadderton where the posh people lived a hundred years ago. He was single, had a spare bedroom and cared more about the desecration of the Carlyle Road Mosque than he did about *Middlemarch* and homework and schoolkid stuff in general. In fact, Ashraf hoped that when things quietened down he might be able to persuade Waseem to let him quit school altogether and work at the garage, which would really be something. Of course there were things to be taken care of first. Things and people, but they'd sort it, him and Waseem. No problem.

SIXTY

That same Saturday, the parents of the late Hanif Qureshi received a letter from a man they'd never heard of. This was not of itself unusual – their dead son's publisher still occasionally forwarded fan mail from readers who had discovered his novel and were unaware that its author was no longer alive. What was unusual was that this letter had not come via the publisher, and it wasn't fan mail. The signature scrawled at the bottom was something or other Fixby – Stanton or Staunton or Stanter or some such. The envelope was postmarked Shadderton, where the couple no longer resided. The contents of the letter were as follows:

Dear Mr and Mrs Qureshi
I've taken the liberty of writing to you because I feel sure that when you gave permission for your late son's name to be linked to that of Alec Bennett as the name of the Millennium Development here in Shadderton, you could not have been aware of a certain fact; namely that Mr Bennett was a racist. In 1952, Bennett wrote a play called The Sun Never Sets. *I doubt you've heard of it – I certainly hadn't – but it's about the son of a maharaja who is being educated at an English public school. It's allegedly a comedy, and I won't bore you with a catalogue of the offensive stuff it contains – you can probably imagine it anyway, so I'll confine myself to a single example. In one scene, the Headmaster receives a telegram informing him that the boy's father – the maharajah – has been taken ill and is not expected to recover. The lad must return to India at once in order to assume the responsibilities his father will shortly relinquish. Having read the telegram, the Headmaster cries, 'Good Lord! That dusky duffer couldn't run an egg and spoon race, let alone a province.'*

Of course it may be that this sort of stuff doesn't offend you at all – all I can say is, I wouldn't want my dead son's name associated with it, especially if he himself had been a bit 'dusky'.

Yours sincerely

SIXTY-ONE

'Steve? Martin. Did you see Saturday's *Post*?'

'Yes, I did.'

'What about Number Two Commando then – brilliant job or what?'

'Uh . . . yeah, but like . . .'

'What? What's your problem, Steve? Can you see the Pakis wanting their kids in the new school after that, with the kids of them that *did* it?'

'No I can't, and that's just it. We've gone too far. They're talking about *killing* people. They mean us. I didn't expect it'd come to this. When I joined Blackout, I mean. I . . . I'm quitting, Martin.'

'Oh you are, are you? You've obviously forgotten Rule One, lad. Rule One says nobody quits Blackout.'

'I never heard of Rule One, or any other rule come to that. Nobody showed *me* any rules.'

'Oh, they're not written down, Steve. Nothing is. Dangerous stuff, writing. But rules are rules and Rule

One is, no quitting. So. What were you thinking of doing tonight?'

'I've got English homework. I'm doing that.'

'No, no, no – that's what you were *thinking* of doing, Steve. Now I'll tell you what you *are* doing, OK?'

'No. No it's not OK, Martin. I don't give a toss about your rules. I'm staying in tonight and you won't see me Friday either. Or any other time. I quit, and that's that.'

'Oh it is, is it? Just like that?' The man sighed. 'You know . . . you disappoint me, laddie, you really do. I had faith in you, unlike some people I could mention. They warned me but I wouldn't listen. That kid, they said. He's a loser. No commitment. No guts. First tight corner, they said, and he'll do a runner on you 'cause he's yellow. That's what they told me, but I thought I knew better. I thought I saw *potential* in you, Steve. Potential officer material, so instead of kicking you out like these people wanted me to, I promoted you. Second in command, Number One Commando. At seventeen. And this – this is how you repay me, by running at the first whiff of danger, just as they said you would. They'll laugh when I tell 'em, Steve. They'll laugh, and then they'll come looking for you. I won't be able to stop 'em, and when they find you they'll do things to you that'll make Khalifa look like a branch of the Samaritans.'

'Who . . . who're you talking about, Martin? Who'll

come looking for me? I'll go to the police. Tell them about the mosque. And the house. I know they'll arrest me too but I don't care.'

'Oh foolish, foolish boy.' Lawson's tone was soft, almost sorrowful. 'You don't understand, do you? The position you're in, I mean. Listen. Suppose a rumour got out? A rumour about somebody having seen a young lass looking quite a lot like your sister, coming out of the butcher's with a funny parcel? A parcel with blood on it. And suppose Khalifa got wind of this rumour? What d'you reckon young Colleen's chances'd be, Steve?'

'You . . . you wouldn't . . .'

'Oh, I promise you I would, laddie. No hesitation whatever. So listen. What's the best method of defence?'

'I–I don't know what you mean, defence. Defence against what?'

'Against anything, Steve. Anyone. The best method of defence is attack. Have you never heard that? It's a very old saying.'

'Y–yes, I think I've heard it, but –'

'I'm glad, because that's exactly how we'll defend ourselves tonight against Khalifa. D'you know that derelict factory on Westgate? Used to be Tatlock's?'

'Yes I do, but –'

'Be there. Eight o'clock sharp. And bring something. A hammer or hatchet.'

'Why? I mean, what for?'

'We're having a car boot sale. Tools. If you can't manage a hammer fetch a screwdriver, only make it a long one. Oh – and if you feel tempted to give it a miss, remember that rumour I mentioned. The one about your sister. See you at eight.'

SIXTY-TWO

'Dad?' The Crowleys were eating their meal. It was six o'clock. Stephen couldn't handle it any more. Not by himself. Two hours and he'd be in the thick of it, whatever it was, and it wouldn't be a car boot sale. If it was just him it'd be bad enough, but now they were threatening Colleen. He didn't know what the heck to do, but Dad might. Michael Crowley looked up and Stephen was framing his first sentence when his sister broke in.

'Guess what?' The way her eyes shone told Stephen she wasn't about to say, 'Stephen's got himself mixed up with this mob called Blackout.' What she did say was, 'School's sending some of us out to work in shops and offices for two weeks, starting next Monday. Abi and I have been chosen. We're off to this firm called Fixby and Walsh.'

Her father frowned. 'I thought this work experience lark was in June or July – just before the summer holiday?'

Colleen nodded. 'Usually it is, but if you remember they couldn't fit everybody in last time. Not enough places. Well, now those of us who missed out are getting our turn. We'll be paid and everything, but the most brilliant bit is me and Abi getting the same firm. Most places only take one.'

'Well, congratulations, love.' Michael grinned ruefully. 'I only hope the world of work doesn't turn out to be less fun than you expect. The novelty certainly wears off after a while, but maybe not in two weeks.'

Stephen tried again. 'Da –'

'And what will you actually be *doing* at Fixby and Walsh, you and Abida?' This from her mother. Stephen sighed.

'I don't really know, Mum. Miss Lackland doesn't know exactly. She mentioned reception work, answering the phone, filing, but they never really know. It's up to the firm.' Colleen smiled. 'She *did* warn us we could end up making coffee for a fortnight, but I wouldn't mind if we did. Better than boring old school.'

Sonia Crowley nodded. 'It'll certainly make a change, darling. I enjoyed working in an office.' She smiled. 'Did I ever tell you about the time my friend and I – Sharon Battersby was her name – wonder what *she's* doing now? Anyway, there was an important client . . .'

Stephen speared a bit of haddock with his fork, lifted it to his mouth and chewed resignedly. Mum's stories always went on for about a thousand years, and anyway he'd gone off telling Dad. It'd cause a terrific row, and what could Dad do anyway, short of locking Colleen in her room for the rest of her life? No, the only thing was to do what Martin wanted. At least his sister would be safe, and maybe a way out would present itself later. He excused himself and went out to the hut to select a screwdriver. Nobody mentioned his uneaten food or asked him where he was going. They were all wrapped up in Colleen's coming adventure. He'd have to face his without them.

Twenty-six men in the dim emptiness of Tatlock's former weaving shed. Twenty-six men, one woman and Stephen, all armed to the teeth. Stephen had been the last to arrive. He'd seen a look pass between Phil and Dean which meant *huh – look who's decided to turn up. Shame we won't get to kick his tripes out and shop his little sister to the Pakis.* Martin Lawson was wearing one of those balaclava masks bank robbers wear in films and carrying a hatchet. He got up on a box and started to speak. Stephen felt unreal, like a character in a play.

'Two blocks from here, the Asian Youth Movement has its HQ. You all know it. Khalifa uses the upstairs room Mondays. They're up there now, plotting how to wipe us out. I've had the place watched and I know there's sixty-one of 'em, which means we're well outnumbered. There are two bits of good news. One, we're armed and they're not. And two, they don't know we're coming. So, here's the plan. When I give the word, Number Three Commando slips out the back of here, picks up stones and moves quietly along the backstreet to the rear of enemy HQ. At eight fifteen precisely, this Commando stones the upstairs windows, creating a diversion. By then the rest of us'll be outside the front door. At the sound of breaking glass we go in and rush the stairs, led by Number One Commando who'll deal with sentries, if any. Then we burst into the room and smash 'em. Three Commando will reach the front via the alleyway and follow us up so we're at full strength. We're going to smash 'em once and for all, before they can do the same to us. Any questions?'

Yes, Stephen thought but didn't say. What the flipping heck am I *doing* here?

SIXTY-THREE

Basir Khan waited till the angry buzz subsided. The assault on the Carlyle Road Mosque had united the Muslim community and the room was packed. The people were demanding revenge. Basir meant to deliver it.

'It is unlikely we shall ever find the individuals who actually carried out this dastardly attack,' he told them quietly, 'but we all know the name of the organization which sent them. Blackout sent them. I hold the members of that organization collectively responsible, and I propose that just retribution be visited on them all.'

At this the audience became noisy again, forcing Khan to pause. He rested his clasped hands on the desktop and gazed calmly at them till his stillness quietened them. 'There is a place – a public house – where Blackout meets. It meets on Friday evenings, which is unfortunate because Friday evenings are for prayer, not bloodletting. However, I have spoken with Imam Salaam, who feels that the wrong we mean to punish far outweighs the wrong we will do in punishing it. Therefore we shall meet this Friday evening at a place to be –'

The three windows of room two imploded simultaneously, bringing Basir Khan's speech to a premature end. His audience, showered with glittering shards, scrambled to its feet with cries of pain and rage. Stones skittered across the dusty floor, their noise masking for a second or two the pounding of boots on the stairway. Before the gathering had time to realize that this was more than a stone-throwing incident, the door burst open. Roaring men in leather jackets poured into the room, swinging hatchets and hammers, slashing and stabbing with knives, chains and screwdrivers. Chairs went over as the room's unarmed occupants scrambled to escape the murderous assault. A few grabbed chairs to use as shields or as weapons, while others protected themselves as best they could with arms and hands. Those who fell, fell on broken glass. Blood smeared the floor and spattered the walls. The stamping, screaming and yelling was easily audible in the street outside. A woman with a toddler stood for a moment amazed, then swept up her infant and ran, not home, but towards the nearest phone box.

SIXTY-FOUR

There had been no sentries. Brian Maxwell had charged the door and gone in with his Stanley knife. Stephen, second man in, had waved his screwdriver about and yelled at the top of his voice, trying to avoid actually hurting anybody. The inward rush of his companions had propelled him into the middle of the room where he'd got his foot entangled in an overturned chair and gone down, slicing open his left palm on a bit of broken glass and falling on the screwdriver, which jabbed into his right side. Trampled and in agony he'd tried to get up, but somebody had swung a chair at his head and he'd dropped senseless to the floor.

Not surprisingly, the fight was going very much Blackout's way when the young mother's phone call brought the police charging up the stairs. Room two looked like a slaughterhouse. It took seventeen officers and four dogs to separate the combatants, and when this was finally done, eleven bodies lay on the spattered floor. A few men had heard the sirens and fled. The rest were restrained and bundled down the dim stairway into waiting vehicles, which moved off quickly to make way for a small fleet of ambulances.

Ashraf, both knees smashed by a lump-hammer, was in great pain as they stretchered him down. In the ambulance on the road to Shadderton Royal Infirmary he was given morphine and at some point he must have passed out, because the next thing he knew he was lying on his back in a narrow bed and a succession of bright lights was passing overhead, like a train. It was a while before he realized that he, not the lights, was moving. Galileo was right, he thought, and giggled. A face appeared, eyes peering into his own. 'OK, old son,' murmured a voice. 'You're going to be just fine.'

He didn't feel fine. Not then, and not when they transferred him from the trolley to a bed and he turned his head and saw another bed about two metres away with a guy in it. The guy's head was in a funny wire contraption like something out of a horror film, but even so he could see it was Stephen Crowley.

SIXTY-FIVE

'Boss? Jenny Most. Could I pop in and see you? Won't take a minute.'

O. B. Stocks grunted. 'What is it? I've a heavy date with the Chief Constable at one.'

'Front Office has sent up a letter. It's from Hanif Qureshi's father. I think you'd want to see it.'

'I can't imagine why, but wheel it in if you must.'

Mobberley
Cheshire
5/10/98

Dear Editor

I enclose a letter my wife and I received yesterday, the purpose of which seems to be to persuade us to withdraw our permission for the use of our late son's name in connection with the Millennium Development. Since we believe that one aim of the development is to weld the multi-ethnic peoples of the town into a single, harmonious community, we thought it might be useful to reproduce this letter in the Post, together with our considered response to it, which is as follows:

Dear Mr – ?

We would like to thank you for your recent letter. We would like to but we cannot, since it displays precisely the sort of prejudice for which it presumes to condemn the late Alec Bennett. As you yourself point out, Mr Bennett's play was written in 1952, when racist attitudes were very much the norm here in Britain. The tragedy is that among some sections of the population at least, these ignorant and outmoded attitudes persist to the present day, causing misery and strife where there might otherwise be peace and harmony.

My wife and I had in fact heard of The Sun Never Sets: *we even saw it, in London in 1954. It was racist by the lights of today but it was funny too, and also quite wise. In short it was the work of a sensitive, intelligent man who, were he alive today, would be writing quite differently. We are proud and happy that our son's name is to be linked with Mr Bennett's, and it is our fervent hope that the Bennett Qureshi Millennium Development might contribute in some small way toward the emergence in the next millennium of a gentler, wiser and more harmonious Britain.*

Peace and love
Sushila and Younis Qureshi

O. B. Stocks studied the scrawled signature which had foxed the Qureshis. He frowned, then smiled. 'Stanton Fixby. I fancy I know what *your* little game is – you had your eye on that town centre site for a nice little earner of your *own*, didn't you? Anyway.' He nodded and pushed the papers across to the woman. 'It's absolutely bang on as far as we're concerned. I'll call Fixby, but we're going with this anyway. Letter *and* response. Front page. And put Fixby's name to his bit.' He grinned. 'Publish and be damned, as somebody or other once said.'

SIXTY-SIX

Brian Maxwell skipped work that Tuesday. He was hurting too much to drive a fork-lift round a timber yard. His head, arms and shoulders were a mass of lumps and bruises, but the bit that hurt most was his feelings. His self-respect. For the first time since primary school, Brian felt humiliated.

It had happened like this. Rampaging through room two last night, swinging and slashing with his trusty blade, he hit a wall with his hand. The impact knocked the weapon out of his grasp, and as he bent to recover it, somebody clouted him with a length of four-by-two.

Because he worked in a timber yard he knew all there was to know about four-by-two *except* what it feels like across the left ear. It hurts.

Straightening up, unarmed, he found himself facing the two mates of the youth whose ear he'd amputated a couple of weeks back. He couldn't understand where they'd got the wood, but they both had five-foot lengths and he could tell by their expressions they *weren't* about to do a bit of DIY, so he did the only thing he could in the circumstances. He turned and ran. That wouldn't have been so bad if his attackers had been satisfied to see him flee, but they weren't.

They chased him down the stairs, through the doorway and all the way along Westgate, clouting him all the time with their makeshift clubs.

And he yelled, and people heard, and saw. Saw *him*, Brian Maxwell, Deputy Commander of Blackout and cock of the Valley Kop, being thwacked by two Pakis along one of Shadderton's busiest streets and howling like a whipped mongrel.

That's why he couldn't show his face at work. *That's* what hurt.

He sat behind the drawn curtains of his frowsty bed-sitting room all that day, brooding. How do you get it back, that self-respect? he wondered. You can always regain the respect of others. That's dead easy. All you do is, you beat the shit out of anyone who mentions the embarrassing incident, or who smirks when it is mentioned, or who smirks in your presence whether it has been mentioned or not. But *self*-respect. That's another matter.

At four o'clock it came to him, how he could get even. He knew where one of those guys lived, because the family had been moved out to Brockbank and Blackout was keeping tabs on everybody involved in that move.

What he'd do was, he'd go over there tonight and burn the guy's house down. *That'd* show him, right? That'd teach him what happens to guys who hit the Deputy Commanders of well-oiled Nazi machines with bits of four-by-two.

Yeah!

SIXTY-SEVEN

'Look . . . er.' Awkwardly, Michael Crowley held out the bag of grapes. 'We brought these for our lad but it turns out he can't eat 'cause his jaw's wired, so we thought . . .' He nodded towards Ashraf, who was talking to his mother.

Hassan Khan took the bag, nodding. 'Thank you, yes.' His wife glanced up at him, then at the stranger. 'Shuk'ran,' she murmured, then lowered her eyes.

Michael looked at Hassan. 'Your son – I hope he's not too badly hurt?'

'Ah – no, Alla ka shuk'r hey. Not too badly. Your boy?'

'Not as bad as it might have been, thank God. Fractured jaw. He'll mend.'

Michael carried a chair round Stephen's bed and sat down. Sonia was already seated at the nearside. Stephen couldn't move his head, and could see his parents only out of the corner of his eyes. Michael bent forward. 'We had the police round this morning. Your mother's very upset. What the heck were *you* doing with a bunch of brain-dead Nazis, smashing up a meeting?'

Stephen tried a shrug, which hurt. Speaking hurt too, and he couldn't do it properly. 'I . . . short of got miksht up wiv 'em, Dad. Couldn't – you know – gerraway. Vey've got waysh of, like, pershuading you, wonsh you're in. Shorry.'

'I should think you *are* shorry, lad, and you might have been a great deal shorrier. Doctor says if it'd been your skull . . .' He let the sentence hang, gazing across his mummified son and his wife's shoulder towards the next bed, where Hassan was bending over Ashraf.

'You will have noticed', Hassan was saying softly, 'that you have received no visit from your cousin Waseem, which shows how good a Muslim *he* is. Perhaps in future you will credit your father with a smattering of intelligence and listen when he tells you that some people are best avoided.'

Ashraf sighed. 'Waseem was *there*, Dad. He's probably lying somewhere in this hospital right now. He could even be dead.'

Hassan shook his head. 'Nobody is dead, Al'ham du'lil'lah, and all of the injured are in this ward. Your cousin's not here and he's not at his work. When you leave hospital you will not return to Waseem's flat. You will live with your mother and sister at Brockbank, or I will send you to Pakistan for a year or two to learn some manners. Those are your choices. Use your time here to ponder them.'

As the fathers of the injured boys were talking none too sympathetically to their sons, O. B. Stocks was taking an equally firm line with Stanton Fixby. '*Take* legal advice, old lad. Take legal advice till you're blue in the face. The fact is, you wrote the letter. You *signed* it, for crying out loud, and I'm publishing it. What'll you say — that it's a forgery? That *I* wrote it? You haven't a leg to stand on and you know it. All I rang you for was to let you know the nature of the Qureshis' response, and to give you the opportunity to make a statement.'

'You have my statement,' grated Fixby. 'It is that if you publish that letter — that *private* letter — I'll take you to the cleaners. I'll wipe you out. When my lawyers

are through, there'll be no such paper as the *Post*. It'll
be history, and so will you.'

'Get stuffed, Fixby,' growled O. B. Stocks, and hung
up.

SIXTY-EIGHT

It was pitch dark and drizzling when Brian Maxwell
turned his old VW and parked, ready for a quick
getaway. He checked his watch: 23.44. The Hussains
would be either in bed or watching some corny old
Bombay epic. In bed would be better, but it is possible
to pour petrol through somebody's letter box while
they're glued to the telly. He checked that nobody was
in sight, lifted the plastic jerrycan off the passenger seat
and got out. He didn't lock the driver's door. There
was an outside chance that somebody might nick the
VW in the few minutes he'd be away, but it wasn't
likely. Not with bigger and better cars standing empty.

Halcyon Way. Who the heck dreams up these flipping street names? Brian wondered. It'll be in the paper
tomorrow, this name. Not mine, though. No chance.

He set off, the heavy can bumping his leg, looking
for number eight. The few houses he passed were in
darkness, and when he spotted the one he wanted, it

was dark too. Next door was lit up like a Christmas tree, but it was going to seem seriously drab in fifteen minutes' time compared to number eight. He glanced about him, saw that Halcyon Way was deserted, and strode up the path.

It was dead easy. Wide letter slot, no spring. He tipped the can. Petrol glugged out, splashing on something soft. Doormat probably. He kept glancing round. Music from next door. Paki music, so *they* won't have minded when Pakis moved in next to them. He smiled at the thought. The can was nearly empty. He couldn't quite tip it enough to get the last drop out. Didn't matter.

He squatted, pulled a grubby duster from his pocket and poured the last of the petrol over it. He ignited a corner with a disposable lighter, straightened up and shoved the duster through the slot. There was a dull roar from inside. The small glass panel in the door grew suddenly bright. Brian stepped back and pocketed the lighter. The can he left where it was. The disposable plastic gloves he wore ensured it bore no prints. He walked down the path and back along Halcyon Way. An old guy was walking a dog. As they passed, Brian looked away to hide his face. The old gimmer'd never remember anyway.

The VW was still there. Who'd want it? He grinned in the drizzly dark. The Hussains might be glad of it tomorrow. They could live in it if the fire didn't get 'em. He slipped in and drove away, his bumps and bruises feeling far less painful than before.

SIXTY-NINE

Brian Maxwell didn't know it, but most of the Hussains were out when he started the fire. They were only next door watching a video so they'd left two-year-old Tasleem fast asleep in her cot upstairs.

It was the old dog-walker who raised the alarm. He was passing number eight when a pane tinkled and the fire stuck its tongue out. He battered on the door of number ten but kids did that every night for fun. It was only when he rapped on the window that somebody came to the door.

They called 999. Tasleem's father, Shabir, went in through the back door and tried to reach his daughter but found the staircase ablaze. Two cousins had to drag him from the doomed house, his hands and scalp badly burned. The brigade reached the scene in nine minutes and a firefighter brought the baby out. They tried mouth-to-mouth resuscitation but she'd inhaled smoke and was dead. Her screaming mother was stupefied with sedatives before being lifted into the ambulance which would rush the two of them, too late, to hospital.

SEVENTY

Wednesday's front page was *not* the one O. B. Stocks had hoped to publish. BABY DIES IN ARSON ATTACK was the headline, over a shot of the gutted house. The police were saying that there was no proof of a racial motive for the attack, but O.B.S. refused to print this without comment. *It is difficult, if not impossible,* he wrote in his editorial, *to imagine any other motive, particularly in view of recent incidents in the town*. He went on to appeal for calm in all quarters, though without much hope. The Shadderton Muslim Association added its voice to this appeal – its spokesman pleaded with 'the men of violence' to let the forces of law and order deal with the tragedy. *Violence breeds violence*, he said, *as we have seen*.

After school that day, Abida and Colleen went together to visit their brothers. The two boys were ignoring each other. The grapes lay untasted on Ashraf's locker and Stephen stared straight ahead, using his injuries as an excuse. Their mutual animosity crackled in the air making the girls feel uncomfortable, though they were determined to dispel it.

Abida placed a chair close to her brother. 'Kya haal hay?'

'I'm OK,' he growled. 'Why are you with *her*?'

'Her brother's in the next bed,' Abida replied, 'in case you hadn't noticed. And because we're friends.'

'Friends? Have you seen today's paper?'

'Of course.'

'And you can call her friend?'

'It's an awful thing. A tragedy. But Colleen's not to blame. Might as well blame the nurse who just walked by.'

'I do.'

'Stupid.'

'They're all responsible, Abi. Thick and ignorant. "Are you a Muzlim?" that one asked me yesterday. She was filling in a form. I said no, I'm a Muslim. *Muzlim* means black. She'd no idea what I was talking about.'

'Oh come *on*, Ash – you can't expect –'

'Why not? Our people have lived here for thirty years, and theirs lived in India for a hundred and fifty. They laugh if a Pakistani pronounces winter "vinter". Why can't *they* learn to pronounce a few basic words properly?'

Abida shrugged. '*Teach* them, Ash. Explain to the nurse. I'm sure she wouldn't mind.'

'She might. They're always right, you see. Always have been, the British. Everybody knows that.'

Colleen was having an equally unrewarding conversation with Stephen. '*Talk* to him,' she was saying. 'Ask him how he's feeling. It's daft, lying next to each other day after day saying nothing. You go to the same school. You're in the same year, studying the same flipping *novel*. Ask him how he's getting on with *Middlemarch*.'

'I don't give a shit how he's getting on with *Middlemarch*, *or* how he's feeling. Look at me, Col. One of his mates did this to me. What about how *I'm* feeling?'

'You went in *armed*, Steve. Started attacking people. What did you expect 'em to do – sit there and let you? You got what you deserve, if you ask me.'

'I didn't ask you.'

'No, well. If you won't talk to him, *I* will. Hey, Ash – how's it going over there? Good opportunity to read some *Middlemarch*, or what?'

There was no reply. Abida said something to her brother and pushed his shoulder, but he refused to look in Colleen's direction. Abida smiled across at her friend. 'My brother says, "I'm feeling much better today, and thank you for asking. And yes, I intend reading the whole of *Middlemarch* while I'm in hospital." You might not have heard him clearly – his injuries have damaged his vocal cords, which are in his legs.'

Colleen giggled. '*My* brother's vocal cords are in the usual place, but his words are muffled by his bandages. He says, "Hi, Ash! I didn't see you there 'cause I can't turn my head. I wish I could, so I could gaze at that gorgeous sister of yours. In between chapters of

Middlemarch, of course." We don't mind relaying your messages, boys. Do we, Abi?'

It was hard work. When after half an hour the girls got up to leave, their brothers still hadn't spoken a word to each other, but Ashraf followed them with his eyes as they walked side by side down the ward. At the doorway they turned and waved. Stephen didn't see this because he couldn't turn his head. As his sister passed from view, Ashraf glanced across. 'They waved,' he growled.

SEVENTY-ONE

'Martin?'

'Yeah. Who's this?'

'Brian.'

'Where the heck have you *been*, Brian? I've been trying –'

'Listen. You've got to help me, Martin. I don't know what to do. How was *I* to know there was a baby in the house?'

'Baby? What baby? You don't mean it was *you* who –'

'Yes, it was me, but I didn't mean it. I wouldn't hurt a baby, Martin. Not a *baby*.'

'You bloody idiot, Brian! You, of all people. I thought you'd more sense. You know what you've done, don't you?'

'Yes, Martin. Killed a kid.'

'Stop whining about *that*, you plonker. I don't give a damn about that. Lost us our funding is what you've done. I got a call first thing this morning, from the guy I met at the Golden Goose. He told me, "No more cash. Killing a kid's like killing a copper," he says, "they'll never rest till they get you and I can't afford to be connected. Goodbye," he says, and hangs up. *That's* what you've done to us, Brian.'

'I–I'm sorry, Martin. I didn't mean . . . they showed me up, see? In front of people. I had to get even.'

'Yes, well you did that all right, and now you're on your own. Blackout didn't order that burning, Brian. In fact, Blackout doesn't *know* anyone called Brian. Do you understand what I'm saying?'

'Martin, please! You can't just –'

'*Can't* I just? You call this number again or let me catch a glimpse of you *anywhere*, and I'll grass you up to that kid's family myself. Goodbye, Brian. Sleep tight.'

SEVENTY-TWO

Friday morning. Stanton Fixby was at the office, a copy of the *Post* spread on his leather-topped desk. His letter to the Qureshis, and their response, dominated the front page. On an inside page, Jennifer Most's column consisted of an interview with a granddaughter of Alec Bennett. Fixby skimmed this and it further fuelled his anger. The woman remembered her grandfather as a gentle, tolerant man who, though busy, always had time for the children. And of course he was the least racist man in England.

The phone rang. Fixby sighed and picked it up. 'Fixby.'

'Have you seen today's *Post*, Stanton?'

'Congratulations, Russell – you're the thousandth caller who's asked me that in the last hour. You win an all-expenses paid weekend for two in Milton Keynes.'

'For goodness' sake, Stanton, this isn't a joking matter. What on earth possessed you to write to the Qureshis? Didn't it occur to you they might give your letter to the press? Can't you see how that Paki-loving buffoon, Stocks, is trying to link you – link *us* – with what certain extremist elements have been up to in Shadderton recently? That *baby*?'

'Chill out, Russell, for God's sake. The letter links us with *nothing*. It's a letter from a private individual who's concerned that a former citizen should have all the facts before taking a decision, that's all. It has nothing to do with violence, and nothing whatever to do with you. I'll say to you what I said to Kenneth Coxmoor when *he* phoned in a panic about nine minutes ago. Everything's fine. O. B. Stocks isn't aware of any link between us. Things are going according to plan. Better, in fact. And as for that arson attack, I've taken steps to ensure we're . . . ah . . . *distanced* from it, shall we say, in case of accidents. All we have to do is sit tight and keep our mouths shut and we'll get the result we want. And now if you don't mind, I've a company to run. Bye.'

SEVENTY-THREE

The thickset man in the biker jacket looked haggard and upset. The desk-constable assumed his helpful expression and said, 'Now, sir – what can we do for you?' He bet the guy's Harley had been nicked.

'I . . .' The man glanced around, leaned over the

counter and spoke quietly. 'I've come to give myself up.'

'Oh, yes? And what exactly is it you've *done*, sir?'

'Eight Halcyon Way. I want to talk to somebody.'

Seconds later, Brian Maxwell was sitting at a table in a bare little room deep in the heart of the station. For the first time since last Wednesday, he felt safe. A cassette recorder winked at him. The Detective Constable seated opposite did not.

'So you were one of those who entered the premises at number nine Westgate last Monday evening with the intention of attacking members of an organization which was holding a meeting there. Is that correct?'

'Yes. It was a Khalifa meeting. They were planning to do us all in, see? We were just defending ourselves, Martin said.'

'Now just a minute. *Planning to do us all in.* Who's *us*, exactly?'

'Blackout. Because of the pig's head.'

'Pig's head. What *is* that — a pub?'

'No — you *know*. The pig's head in the mosque.'

'Ah!' The officer nodded. 'So that was Blackout, was it? You mentioned someone called Martin just now. Who's Martin?'

'Martin Lawson of course. He *invented* Blackout. God, don't you guys *read* the papers?'

The detective gave Brian a stony stare. 'I'm asking the

questions, you're answering. Unless of course you're ready to leave. You're not under arrest, you know. You're free to go at any time.'

'No,' groaned Brian, shaking his head. 'I'm not free. I don't *want* to be free. I haven't shut my eyes for five bleeding nights. All I want to do is get it off my chest and crash out in a nice, safe cell where they can't get to me.'

'Who?'

'Khalifa, of course. They don't screw around you know, those guys. There's Cardigan Street. There's the pig's head, and now there's Halcyon Way. I torched it. The whole world's going mad on the Millennium, and I'll be lucky if I live to *see* it.'

'Ah, right.' The detective nodded and leaned back in his chair. 'Halcyon Way. Yes.' He sighed. 'Brian Heinrich Himmler Maxwell, I'm arresting you for the murder of Tasleem Hussain. You're not obliged to say anything, but . . .'

SEVENTY-FOUR

Martin Lawson ran his own estate agency from premises near the town centre. He was running his eyes down the 'Appointments to View' list on the monitor when

Karen stuck her head round the door. 'Two gentlemen to see you, Mr Lawson.'

'I've no appointment listed for two o'clock, Karen. What do they want?'

'I doubt they make appointments, Mr Lawson. They're from the police.'

'Police?' Martin fiddled with the keyboard to hide his apprehension. 'Did they say what it was about at all?'

'No. Just they wanted a word. Shall I show them in or what?'

'Yes, I . . . suppose you'd better. And then make some coffee.

'Good afternoon, sir. I'm Detective Sergeant Barraclough and this is D.C. Thompson. We'd like a few minutes of your time, if it's quite convenient.'

'Yes. Yes of course. Won't you sit down? The girl's making coffee if you'd like some.'

'No thank you, sir. We want to talk to you about a group known as Blackout, which we understand you founded.'

'That's right, sergeant, I did. It's a political organization.' He shrugged modestly. 'Just local, you know.'

'Yes, we know. We entertained several of your members down at the station last Monday night. They're out on bail. Three others are detained in Shadderton General. A somewhat *lively* political organization, wouldn't you say?'

Lawson shrugged. 'We . . . like to get our point of view across, sergeant, and it's hard graft getting through to some people.'

'Ah-ha. And that's why you carry hatchets and hammers into the debating chamber, is it? In order to get *through*, as it were?'

'Oh, we don't encourage that sort of thing, sergeant. No, no. Not in Blackout. Of course, it happens now and then that a few of our more hot-headed members get carried away and do things that tend to sully our reputation.' He smiled. 'Occasionally it becomes necessary to discipline them.'

Barraclough sighed. 'Your discipline wasn't terribly impressive in that meeting room, but then you didn't stay around to apply it, did you, Mr Lawson? Did a runner when you heard the sirens, I expect.'

'Oh no, sergeant. You've got it all wrong. I wasn't present on that occasion. It wasn't a sanctioned operation, you see.'

'Oh now come *on*, Mr Lawson. You surely don't expect us to swallow that?'

Lawson's brow rose. 'Did any of those you . . . entertained *say* I was there, sergeant?'

'No sir, they didn't.'

'Well then.' Lawson sat back smiling. 'There's nothing to connect me with the incident, is there? No evidence.'

The detective shook his head. 'I didn't say that, sir.

I said none of those we *arrested* put you at the scene. However, somebody else *did*.'

'Who? Who said I was there? Whoever he is, he's a liar.'

'Does the name Maxwell ring a bell, Mr Lawson? Brian Maxwell?'

Lawson frowned and shook his head. 'No. Never heard of him.'

'Well, you know that's odd, because Mr Maxwell claims he's second in command of Blackout.'

'He's mad. I have no second in command. This fellow, whoever he is, knows nothing. Nothing.'

'He knows a bit about pigs' heads, Mr Lawson. And mosques. He keeps going on about Cardigan Street too, *and* Halcyon Way. Seems to think *you* know about those things as well. Blabbers on about Khalifa, and not living to see the Millennium. Oh, by the way –' The sergeant gazed into Lawson's eyes. '– one of those places he talks about. Halcyon Way. A child died there in an arson attack which Maxwell says you planned. That's murder, Mr Lawson.'

Martin Lawson paled. 'He's a damned liar! He did that one by himself. Phoned me, pleading for help. I blew him out and this is his way of getting even. I'm no murderer, sergeant.'

'Tut-tut-tut.' Barraclough shook his head sadly. 'Seems you've been telling me porkies, Mr Lawson. Less than a minute ago you said you'd never *heard* of

Brian Maxwell, now here you are getting phone calls from him and blowing him out. What *am* I to believe, eh? That he's lying? That *you* are? Don't you think it's time to come clean? Child murderers have a rough ride in prison, Mr Lawson. No girls to fetch coffee or anything like that, and we're talking about *life*.'

Coffee came, and was sent away. Martin Lawson began talking to the sergeant as though the policeman might be about to buy a million pound mansion. The only thing he didn't mention was the meeting he'd had a few weeks ago with a certain gentleman at the Golden Goose. Not that he was *protecting* the gentleman or anything like that. He was saving him for later, that's all. Knowledge is power, and Martin had the feeling he was going to need all the power he could muster.

SEVENTY-FIVE

As Martin Lawson was helping the police with their inquiries, Abida and Colleen were being introduced to the world of work. At nine that morning the girls had arrived in their smartest outfits at the Fixby and Walsh building, and had been placed under the wing of Ms Wilkinson, the Office Supervisor. The building was a large one, and Ms Wilkinson had begun with a whirlwind tour. The youngsters were shown reception, the hospitality area, the mail room, records, accounts, the directors' suite, the general office, the lift, the staff staircase, the washrooms, the kitchen, their assembly point in case of fire and about six million other places they knew they'd never find again. Since then, Colleen had spent most of her time making tea and coffee in the kitchen, taking it down the staff stairs to the hospitality area and washing-up. The trays she had to carry, laden with pots and cups and saucers and plates of fancy biscuits, were heavy. She must *never* use the lift, and she must keep the tray level when descending the staircase so as not to slop tea. If she *did* spill anything – anything at all – she must on no account continue. Visitors to Fixby and Walsh were *never* presented with trayfuls of slops. At the slightest mishap she was to return to the kitchen and remove every trace of the spillage before taking down the tray. And if whoever was entertaining the visitor then snapped at her for taking so long, she was to apologize in a mild voice. *Sorry, sir, or ma'am – it won't happen again.* Not, *well it's not my flipping fault is it, traipsing up and down them ruddy stairs all day?* Anything of *that* sort, said Ms Wilkinson, and she'd be sent back to school with a note for the Head.

Abida was a little more lucky. She was put in charge of a sort of trolley on rubber wheels, which she had to push along carpeted corridors. She was to look into

SEVENTY-SIX

If the girls were fed up with work after half a day, their brothers were totally arsed off after a week in hospital. The grub wasn't up to much for a start, plus being bedridden meant there was no way they could escape the daily lectures of their parents. They had to lie there and take it. Also the nurses weren't all that friendly after the body of little Tasleem was brought in. They knew, of course, that the actual arsonist wasn't among their patients, but they'd a fair idea the baby's death was connected in some way with the violence these young men had been involved in. They did their job, but they didn't stay around to chat.

The only good thing, apart from the gradual healing of their wounds, was that the animosity between patients was thawing. It was a slow thaw, but it was definitely happening. Ashraf decided it had something to do with the fact that everybody was in the same boat, and that when you sleep two metres away from somebody for a week, you can't go on believing he's a member of an alien species. You needed the bedpan just as often as he did, and stunk up the ward in exactly the same way. He ate, slept, snored and farted like you did. He had folks who cared about him and came to visit, so had you. They even brought the same *stuff*, for Pete's sake – grapes and Lucozade. Everybody's locker top was crammed with grapes and Lucozade.

That Monday, when all the visitors had gone, Ashraf said, 'Hey, Steve?'

Stephen, who could now turn his head a bit, did so. 'Yeah?'

'Wanna buy some Lucozade?'

'Piss off – have you *seen* the top of my locker?'

'Some grapes, then?'

'No thanks. I wouldn't mind a bit of that curry your mum brings you though.'

'Got anything to trade?'

'Oh yeah – I'm no scrounger.'

'What you got?'

'Grapes. Lucozade.'

'Dipstick. Anyway it's Paki grub. I didn't think you'd want to touch it.'

'I've got to smell it so I might as well eat it. And anyway, it's got to be better than the slop they give us in here.'

So Ashraf shared his meal with Stephen, and both boys spent some time that night lying awake, thinking about the situation they'd let others drag them into, and how daft it was all starting to seem. Neither knew the other was thinking this and they never talked about it, but from that night on their fractured friendship began healing along with their other wounds.

SEVENTY-SEVEN

After lunch, which they ate at a nearby Lite-bite, the two girls returned to their work. It was two o'clock. Colleen went to the kitchen to wash crockery, Abida to Ms Wilkinson's cubicle, outside which she'd parked her trolley. She was passing Mr Fixby's door as his phone rang.

Beyond the door, Fixby picked up. 'Fixby.'

'Stanton, it's Kenneth. Listen. They've arrested that bloody estate agent, Lawson. He's down at the station now, spilling his guts.'

'How d'you know?'

'Liz works there. Computers.'

'Who the devil's *Liz*?'

'My daughter. They've got the guy terrified over that kid at Brockbank. He'll give 'em the lot, including his meeting with you, the money, everything. We're finished.'

'Rubbish! There were no witnesses to that meeting. It's his word against mine. Who d'you think they'll believe – the millionaire property developer, or a crackpot estate agent who thinks he's Hitler?'

'Yes OK, but what about records? You've got stuff written down, I *know* you have. They'll come to your place with a warrant. Rip the place apart. They could be on their way *now*.'

'Relax, Kenneth, or you'll die of a heart attack before they've *time* to throw you in jail. Listen. I'm not a fool. There *are* records, but there are also shredders. In five minutes' time there'll be absolutely nothing. Just make sure *you've* been as careful. You and the others.'

'We never wrote things down, you know that. I'll hang up now so you can get that stuff destroyed. I'll be in touch.'

'No, Kenneth, you won't. We hardly know each other, you and I. Understand?'

'Oh – oh yes. Goodbye then.'

'Bye, Kenneth. Oh, and Kenneth?'

'Yes?'

'Don't imagine all is lost. I fancy things have gone too far to mend. You mark my words – there'll be no Bennett Qureshi Millennium Development.'

Stanton Fixby hung up and touched an intercom pad. 'Oh, Janice. Stanton. Have one of your girls bring the shredder along, will you? Straight away, please. Thanks.' He stood up, strode across to the filing cabinet, withdrew a slim folder and stood, waiting for the girl to knock and enter.

SEVENTY-EIGHT

'Ah, Abida.' Ms Wilkinson stuck her head out of her cubicle. 'On your way round, will you collect the NORDEV file from the general office?'

'NORDEV?'

'Yes. Any of the girls will get it out for you. Shall I write it down, or will you remember?'

'NORDEV. I'll remember.'

'Good girl.'

As she trundled her trolley along the corridor, Mr Fixby's door opened and the Managing Director stuck his head out. He looked furious. Ms Wilkinson had warned Colleen and herself about the MD that morning. 'He's all right is Mr Fixby,' she'd murmured, 'if you keep on the right side of him, but he's got a bit of a temper and can't abide inefficiency. Never, never go into his office without knocking – he's sacked more than one poor girl on the spot for doing that.'

Now he glared at Abida. 'Are you the girl with that damned shredder?'

Abida shook her head. 'N-no, sir.'

'Well, where the bloody hell *is* she, then?' he roared, spit flying from his lips.

Abida shook her head. 'I-I dunno, sir. I –'

'Oh!' The man shook his head in exasperation and stormed off along the corridor, leaving his door open. Glancing in, Abida noticed that there was something in the OUT tray. Might as well take it, she told herself. Better than knocking later, with him in that mood. She glanced along the corridor to make sure he wasn't on his way back, darted inside and grabbed what was in the tray. It was a green folder. She hurried out, and was about to drop it in the file compartment when she noticed the name on the tag. NODEV – the very file Ms Wilkinson was waiting for. No point carrying it all round, she thought. I'll take it straight back to her. She grinned. Brownie point for initiative, maybe.

Ms Wilkinson shook her head. 'This isn't the one, dear. Look.' She showed the tag. 'NODEV. I said NORDEV, with an R. I offered to write it down, but you said –'

'Yes, I'm sorry, Ms Wilkinson. I only glanced at it. I should have –'

'Who *gave* you this?' The supervisor was flicking through the file. 'I've never seen this before. Khalifa? What's that, a company? And Blackout. This looks like Mr Fixby's writing.'

Abida swallowed. Khalifa? Blackout? What were

those names doing on file at Fixby and Walsh? She nodded. 'It was in his OUT tray. I thought it was the one you wanted, so I brought it straight here.'

The woman looked at her. 'Mr Fixby gave it to you?'

'N-no. He went out. Left his door open. I saw it in the tray. Have I done something wrong?'

Ms Wilkinson shook her head. 'I don't know, child. These are records of meetings with people I've never heard of, payments to companies with . . .' She closed the file. 'This can only be something personal of Mr Fixby's. You'd better take it straight back. If he's in, tell him I told you to clear his OUT tray. I don't think he can have meant to put it in there, but he'll realize you were only doing as you'd been told.'

Abida took the file and hurried along the corridor, praying that the MD had not returned. She was halfway there when some words of her brother's came back to her. Funding. Ash had boasted a week or two ago that Khalifa was about to get funding. Serious funding from important people. Funding which would enable the group to expand its operations, get experts in, stuff like that. She stopped, gazing at the green folder. *Meetings with people I've never heard of. Payments to companies . . .* She was cold suddenly. Shivering. What if . . . ? She walked on, past Fixby's open door, heading for the kitchen.

Colleen was wiping a saucer. She stared at her friend.

'What's up, Abi? You look scared to death. Have they sacked you or what?'

Abida shook her head. 'This file. It's got stuff in about Blackout, Col, and Khalifa. Meetings. Payments. Ms Wilkinson says she's never –'

'Payments?' Colleen's mouth gaped. She put down the saucer and tea towel. 'Stephen said somebody was supporting Blackout. Big bucks, he said. You don't think . . . ?'

Abida nodded. 'It's *got* to be, hasn't it? Look – even the name.' She held up the folder. 'NODEV. No development, d'you reckon? That's what it's all about, isn't it? Smashing the Bennett Qureshi Development? I think we should get this to the police, Col. Now.'

'Oh, shit!' Colleen chewed her lip. 'What if we're wrong, though? What if we do a runner with this file and it's something completely innocent? We'll be expelled from school. We'll never get work experience again.' She giggled wildly. 'We'll never get *work*. Are you sure, Abi? I mean . . .'

Abida nodded. 'I'm sure enough to risk it, Col, but it's got to be now. This guy – the MD – he'll be looking for this right now. He'll be looking for *me*. You don't have to come if you don't want to, but I'm off.'

'Don't talk daft.' Colleen tore her pinny off, flung it in a corner. 'Come on – staff staircase.'

★

They'd reached the top step when a voice behind them roared, 'Stop *right* there, you two. That's company property you're stealing!'

SEVENTY-NINE

They were four floors up. The staff staircase connected each floor with the next by means of thirty-two steps arranged in four flights of eight, with quarter landings at each turn. You went down eight steps, turned left, went down eight more, left again and so on. The staircase was built around the shaft of the hoist. As the two girls scampered down the first eight and turned, they heard the clash of a metal door above them.

'He's in the hoist!' gasped Colleen. '*We* should've taken it – he'll be waiting at the bottom.'

'Not if we beat him to the next floor,' cried Abida. 'Come on!' They bounded down, turned, bounded again. The hoist's machinery clanked into motion. 'He's coming!' sobbed Colleen. 'We'll never make it.'

Abida hit the second floor ahead of her friend. The hoist door was still closed. She smacked the call button with the heel of her hand as Colleen skidded round the turn. 'It'll stop here now,' she panted. 'He can't prevent it. Come *on*.' They heard the motor slow to a halt as they continued down. The door would open automatically. Would Fixby take to the stairs or hit the close button and ride? He'd be faster than them on the stairs. They hoped he'd ride.

He wasn't that thick. As they reached the first floor they heard him pounding after them. One more floor. Four more sets of eight, then a short dim corridor and out the back way. Once on the street he could hardly tackle them, but could they stay ahead till then? They plunged on down and he came roaring after, closing the gap. As they leapt the last three steps and hit the corridor, he had them in sight. 'Come back!' he panted. 'That's confidential stuff you're stealing. I'm warning you – you'll go away for *years*.'

The double doors were closed but there was a panic-bar. Abida flung herself against it and the doors burst outwards. They were in a damp, concrete yard with a van and some wheelie bins. Gasping and sobbing the fugitives pelted across the yard, through a gateway and along the side of the building. The street was there in front of them, the MD at their heels. Colleen was finished. She couldn't run another metre. 'Abida!' she cried. 'Not the police, the *Post*. You know who.' She slowed. A large hand grabbed her hair, swung her round. She wrapped both her thin arms round Fixby's flabby one and clung on. Cursing, he tried to shake her off. Abida had reached the street. She looked back, hesitated. 'Go on, Abi!' croaked Colleen, clinging to the damp shirtsleeve. 'Do it.' Fixby swung a punch. It was his left and it only glanced off her cheek but it made her let go. She leaned against the side of the building, bent over, holding her face as he staggered the few metres to the street. He stood panting, glaring along the road but the girl had gone. He turned and came back, with weary steps, to Colleen.

'Where's she gone, eh?' He'd scarcely the breath to speak. 'Where's she taken that folder?'

Colleen straightened up. There were tears, and the beginning of a bruise on her cheek. She shook her head, sniffling. 'I dunno.'

'Of *course* you know. What did you mean, not the police, the post?'

'I meant she should post it.'

'Post it to whom, for heaven's sake, and *why*? What d'you imagine you found, you stupid child?'

'To someone we know. And as to what we imagine, we imagine we found something you'd rather we hadn't.'

'It's a private file, that's all. It's of no interest to anybody but me. You realize you're in serious trouble, don't you?'

Colleen looked at him. 'I think *you* are, Mr Fixby. I'm only in trouble if I'm wrong.'

He snorted. 'You're nothing but a silly, stupid little girl who thinks she's in a spy thriller or something.' He paused. 'Look – I was young once myself, so I'm going to give you one last chance. Go after your friend, bring that folder back and we'll say no more about it. How's that?'

Colleen knuckled her eyes. Fixby fished in his pocket and handed her a Kleenex. 'I'm sorry I was a bit rough just now,' he said. 'I've a bit of a temper, I'm afraid. Now – what d'you say?'

Colleen nodded. If that file was what Abida thought it was, this guy must be pretty desperate. She needed to get away. 'OK, if you promise you won't get the police on to us. You won't, will you?'

'I told you – we'll say no more about it.' He shook his head. 'I hope for both your sakes your friend hasn't posted it already. Off you go, and I want that folder *today*. I'll be in my office till six.'

'Six,' murmured Colleen. That's right – you wait in your office, you fat crook, she thought. Don't go away. I know some people who'll be pretty keen to talk to you. Aloud she said, 'Yes, OK. I'll catch Abida and come right back.'

EIGHTY

'I need to see Jennifer Most,' said Abida breathlessly. The woman behind the counter raised her eyebrows.

'Oh you do, do you? Is Ms Most expecting you?'

'No.'

'Well, I'm afraid you can't just arrive out of the blue and expect a busy person like Ms Most to drop everything and –'

'She interviewed my parents,' interrupted Abida. 'For *Most in the Post*. I'm Abida Khan, and it's urgent.' She wondered what was happening to Colleen.

'Are you, and is it? Well, I'll tell her you're here, but I can't promise she'll see you.'

'Say it's about Khalifa.'

Jennifer Most was there in under a minute. She held up a hand to stem Abida's agitated gabble, steered her into the lift and up to her office. 'Now,' she smiled, when they were both seated, 'take your time, and tell me all about it.'

'It's this, Ms Most.' She slid the green folder across the desk. 'We took it from Fixby and Walsh's, me and

Colleen. It seems to be about Khalifa and Blackout. We were going to take it to the police, but Colleen shouted me to bring it to you. She got caught, you see.'

The journalist's cheeks paled as she flicked through the folder. She glanced up. 'Caught? By whom, Abida?'

'By Mr Fixby. He chased us down the stairs. I took the file from his OUT tray, you see.'

'This . . .' Jennifer indicated the folder, 'if this is genuine, it's absolute dynamite. It seems these guys – Fixby, Coxmoor, Pollinger – are involved in some sort of conspiracy to sabotage the Millennium Development. They've been funding acts of terrorism. There's an Asian businessman involved as well.'

Abida fidgeted on her chair. 'What about Colleen, Ms Most? Mr Fixby was *really* mad. I'm worried in case he –'

'Of course you are. Just a minute.'

Jennifer Most picked up the phone, contacted Police Headquarters and asked for an officer by name. She spoke briefly to this officer, mentioning Colleen, Fixby and the folder. She listened for a moment, nodded and hung up. Abida had watched anxiously throughout. Jennifer smiled. 'It's all right, dear. Seems somebody else has been mentioning Fixby's name down at the station, so the folder's probably genuine. It's going to provide some pretty damning evidence too, unless I'm very much mistaken. In fact, I suppose I *ought* to take it straight to the police.' She winked. 'But my boss'd never forgive me if he didn't get a peep . . .'

The phone rang. The reporter picked up. 'What? *Another* little girl? What's her . . . ? Colleen Crowley. Yes, as a matter of fact I *am* expecting her, Mrs Bostock. Perhaps you'd be good enough to show her the way? Thank you *so* much.' She hung up and beamed at a smiling Abida. 'So you see – your troubles are over.' She pulled a face. 'Let's pray the same can be said for Shadderton.'

EIGHTY-ONE

23.00 hours, 31 December. The year 2000 is drawing to a close. It is a fine evening – cold, but cloudless. A group of friends is making its way towards the rounded summit of Shadderton Hill. The lights of the town lie far below: necklaces of diamond, pearl and amber, strewn on black velvet. The hillside is thronged already with townspeople, and more are arriving all the time. The friends pass a vendor selling the *Post*. 'Souvenir Edition!' he cries, holding a copy aloft. 'Shadderton Gets it Right!'

Stephen grins at his sister. 'D'you remember me saying back in ninety-eight that two thousand was the last year of the *old* Millennium, not the beginning of the new?'

Colleen nods. 'I remember. You said the whole world had it wrong except Stephen Crowley.'

'Actually I think it was *you* said that, but anyway I *was* right. That headline should read, "Stephen Crowley gets it right." Shadderton would've celebrated a year ago with everybody else if they'd finished the development in time.'

'Well, actually, of course,' smiles Abida, 'they'd a lot more time than they knew – it's another five hundred and eighty-one years to the millennium if you go by *our* calendar.'

'So you see, big-head,' growls Ashraf, 'you don't know everything after all. I don't think I should *let* you go on seeing my sister.'

'Hoo!' cries Abida. 'You've no choice, big brother. Dad's quite happy about it.' She grins. 'One peep out of you and he'll send you to Pakistan to learn some manners.'

Ashraf shakes his head. 'You're never going to let me forget that are you, Abi?'

The girl chuckles. 'Never.'

23.30. The four friends, on vacation from their various colleges and universities, sit huddled in coats and scarves, hugging their knees. Ashraf's knees still hurt him a bit now and then, in cold weather. Other groups are all around. There are a few familiar faces. Justin Case is with his new wife and her parents. He sells insurance. Stephen whispers to Abida that his name exactly suits his profession. Old Greenglass is there with two little kids. Grandchildren probably. Ashraf smiles in the dark, remembering *Middlemarch* in A level English lessons. Not far away, sharing soup from a thermos, sit Karim, Rehana and Shofiq Majid. The scar on Rehana's chin has faded with time, and is quite invisible in the dark.

23.50. The last knot of stragglers finds a space and crams itself in. People are standing up. Ten minutes to the fireworks, and to the Millennium. Everybody is there.

Well, no – not everybody. Stanton Fixby isn't, for a start. He's still got seven of his ten years to serve. So have Kenneth Coxmoor and Russell Pollinger. Conspiracy to cause explosions. Martin Lawson's out, but he daren't show his face in Shadderton. He sells houses down south and runs a group called White is Right. Some people never learn.

Jennifer Most is absent. Her coverage of the Shadderton Conspiracy Trial has given her a taste for investigative journalism. She's in London, working for the BBC.

Basir Khan escaped trial by flying on a one-way ticket to Pakistan where, only months later, he suffered a horrible death from hydrophobia after being bitten by a rabid dog. No airline flies where Allah cannot reach.

Brian Maxwell is not on Shadderton Hill either. Adjudged unfit to plead to a charge of murder, he is detained indefinitely at an institution for the criminally insane. There, day and night, the poor fellow roams the spacious grounds, never still, never at rest. Every few paces he glances over his shoulder as if anticipating an attack upon his person, though the institution is ringed by the most advanced security system in Europe. Someday, many years from now, Brian will find his rest. He will find it in a long, pale box buried deep in the earth. In the meantime though, he will walk, and walk, and walk.

23.59. A buzz of excitement under the bright, cold stars. Somebody starts counting down. A hundred voices join in. Fathers lift small children on to their shoulders. Every eye is fixed on the town below. Five, four, three, two, one, ZERO! The sky fills with multicoloured explosions: the lights first, then the noise. A bombardment spectacular enough to drive gasps from the most cynical and to set toddlers whimpering. And below, simultaneously, as if it mirrors the sky, a patch at the centre, black till now, bursts into gorgeous coruscation and there it lies – the Bennett Qureshi Development: Shadderton's gateway to the third millennium, its shape picked out in a horde of blazing gemstones.

As the pyrotechnic boom recedes, the space it leaves is flooded by the cheering of eighty thousand voices. All over the hill people are turning to one another, arms wide to embrace. Helpless with laughter and blind with tears, Abida, Stephen, Colleen and Ashraf stagger, clamped together, sideways across the slope, the night and the cold forgotten.